Divi

Divining Venus

Mary Elizabeth Pope

Joe —
So wonderful to finally
meet you — I cannot thank
you + everyone at Waywiser
enough for your support
of my work.
Best wishes —
Mary Pope

WAYWISER

First published in 2013 by

THE WAYWISER PRESS

Bench House, 82 London Road, Chipping Norton, Oxon OX7 5FN, UK
P. O. Box 6205, Baltimore, MD 21206, USA
http://waywiser-press.com

Editor-in-Chief
Philip Hoy

Senior American Editor
Joseph Harrison

Associate Editors
Dora Malech Eric McHenry Clive Watkins Greg Williamson

A CIP catalogue record for this book is available from the British Library

ISBN 978-1-904130-55-0

Printed and bound by
T.J. International Ltd., Padstow, Cornwall, PL28 8RW, UK

For my parents, Betty and Joe Pope,
for their love, support and stories.

And for my husband, Matt Elliott, who keeps
me anchored to the planet every single day.

Some of these stories have been published previously, in slightly different form:

"Junior Lifesaving" in *Fugue*, Spring 2005.
"Rebound" in *Sycamore Review*, Fall 2006.
"Divining Venus" in *Florida Review*, Spring 2007.
"Boston Cream Pie" in *Descant*, Spring 2009.
"The Score" in *Dos Passos Review*, Spring 2010.
"The Marionette Theater" in *Ascent*, Fall 2010.
"Reunion" in *Upstreet*, Spring 2011.
"The Drill" in *Crab Creek Review*, Fall 2011.
"Personal Space" in *Passages North*, Spring 2012.
"Say Goodbye to Hollywood" in *Ampersand Review*, Spring 2012.
"Endless Caverns" in *Bellingham Review*, Fall 2012.
"The Club" in *PoemMemoirStory*, Spring 2013.
"Moulting" in *Evening Street Review*, Spring 2013.

Contents

Acknowledgments

My sincerest thanks to Philip Hoy at Waywiser, as much for his enthusiastic support of this collection as for his keen editorial eye. I am so grateful to have worked with an editor who has delivered his observations about my work with such care, and who is as insightful as he is kind.

I am also grateful to my agent Ann Collette, whose belief in this collection strengthened my own, and whose effort on my behalf has been generous beyond all expectation.

I'd also like to thank the editors of the literary magazines who published stories from this collection, in particular Ben George at *Fugue*, who accepted the first short story I ever wrote, as well as the late, great Jeanne Lieby, who called to accept the title story for publication in *Florida Review* and told me to never give up.

I owe a tremendous debt of gratitude to many former mentors and colleagues, first and foremost, Robert Root, Jr., as well as Susan Schiller at Central Michigan University; Bill Davis, Jeana Del Rosso and Gene Farrington at College of Notre Dame of Maryland; and my current colleagues at Emmanuel College, too numerous to name, whose enthusiasm for my work saw me through to the finish line.

Many thanks to writers and friends who supported my work on this book in various ways: Sheri Booker, Jean Harper, Donald Lystra, Carole and Michael Steinberg, Kathleen Stocking, as well as

Katie Adam, Greg Bales, Kris Cann, Elizabeth Fels, Rachel Foster, Mary Hayes, Kathy Lyons, Ed Mallot, Eleanor Nickel, Rose Shenk, and my faithful reader and dear friend, June Powell.

My most sincere thanks to my parents, who made storytelling a huge part of my daily life growing up, and who never laughed when I said I wanted to be a writer. My mother still keeps all the hand-stitched, crayon-lettered books I wrote back in grade school, and I'm so glad to finally add a real one to her collection. Thanks, too, to my little sister Jodie Morrison, whose arrival introduced the concept of intentional humor to our family (the rest of us are funny, but not on purpose). I'd also like to thank my mother-in-law, Georgia Elliott, who scoops up whatever I've been writing the minute she walks though the door and reads it all in one go while I pray for her approval.

It is impossible to quantify my gratitude to Matt Elliott, my best friend, husband, colleague, rock and resident comedian, who is my first and last reader, who always tells me the truth about my writing no matter how badly he knows it might end for him, and whose suggestions have made these stories infinitely stronger. Living with a writer can't be easy, and I'm immensely fortunate that he does so with such great love, generosity and equanimity.

Finally, a last note of thanks to teachers Pat Seiter at Mt. Pleasant High School, Sr. Thaddeus Kowalinski at Sacred Heart Academy, and Marge Sheppard, my first grade teacher at Kinney School, who wrote at the bottom of my otherwise unimpressive final report card, "Mary Beth, keep writing your stories."

Reunion

When it come in the mail that day, I couldn't hardly believe it. Just stood there at the end of the driveway with that little square of paper in my hands, a list of names of all those folks I'd lost track of and the date coming right up. But what got me was the twenty-five year part. I mean, in all that time I just moved fifty miles away, and here's twenty-five years, gone.

Some of those names jump right out at me – *Samuel F. Miller, Ronald K. Fuller, Lucinda A. Moore, Marjory L. Simms* – even if I used to know them by others: Sam, Ron, Lucy, Marge. Except Marge, I haven't seen the others in just about the twenty-five years it says on that invitation, and for a second I think how nice it would be to catch up after all these years.

But reunions are for people who got something snappy to show for all that time – a la-di-da car, a split-level house, jeans the same size you wore back then. That's not me. And it's not just the weight. Around my hips now, but there in my face too. Not that I look in the mirror much. Not like I used to. I got two deep lines between my eyebrows showed up after Eddie left and ruined my looks, or what was left of them after having babies, and after a while I just gave up and stopped trying. Them creams don't do nothing but make your lines deeper, what with worrying how you're gonna pay for what they cost.

My maiden name's there on that invitation too: *Patricia R.*

Lapone, it says. I look at that name there in black lettering and try to remember the girl I used to be. That girl thought the world was stretched out in front of her with possibilities, like items you could pick from a cafeteria line. That girl thought you chose your own path in life. She didn't know how sometimes the path chooses you, and no matter how hard you try you can't seem to make your feet go a different way, almost like the path was there long before you came to walk it, long before you were born, even.

Days pass, and I've good and forgotten about that reunion when the phone rings one afternoon, which is rare. I mean, my daughter Marie calls in the evenings when the baby's asleep, and my son Jack only calls once a week since he left for junior college, usually Saturday mornings, wanting money or asking what do I do for a headache? So I already know something's up when I answer, and sure enough, it is.

Now, like I say, Marge is the only friend I still see from high school, and even her I don't see much more than once in a great long while for whiskey sours at the Shepherd Bar, but the second I pick up that phone she starts in about how we have got to get ourselves down to the Dress Barn before that reunion. She says Randy Sanders just got divorced, and since I'm single and so is she, why don't we go together and be each other's dates?

I say, "Marge, I can't go." That is all I can manage. I don't know how to tell her the rest.

Marge says, "Patty, I have had dreams about that man since I was fifteen years old. I will not lose my chance now."

Now, I want to talk her out of this. It seems silly, all these years later, putting so much stock in something somebody used to be twenty-five years ago. But all the time I am thinking this, I can almost feel the way I used to swing my ponytail when I wanted someone whose name is also on that invitation to look my way: *Bernard P. Goodwin.* Benny was a good boy, sweet. I was trouble, couldn't help myself. I used every trick I knew to make Benny love me in those days and it worked. Back in high school that boy adored me. Flat-out worshipped the ground I walked on, like they say. And I thought he was fine, and we went together for years, and Benny took me on dates in his father's Cadillac and sent roses every Tuesday and refused to lay a hand on me until he'd paid for the diamond ring he had on layaway so we could get married in the Maple Street Chapel, but for some reason I had it in my head that love meant running down the beach together naked with a movie soundtrack playing in the background, and there was this bartender worked at McGraw's used to serve me underage who looked at me like he knew that same stretch of beach, and before my nineteenth birthday, I'm knocked up. That was Eddie.

Now, I always thought I'd grow up to be a stewardess and fly to the places in those *National Geographic*s I used to read in doctor's offices. I wanted to wear one of those navy blue get-ups with the white collars and carry my life in one of those neat rolling suitcases. But I had to put all my energy into Eddie after that – cook for him, clean, iron his clothes, keep the kids quiet and out of his way, fix him Sloppy Joes once a week because that's what he loved. And somehow it was like I just disappeared into all that responsibility. Just plain vanished. Sometimes when the kids were at a sleepover I'd put candles on the table and think maybe in the dimmer light Eddie might look at me the way he used to, but he never did, not even once after Marie was born. And he took it all with him when he went, all that time I poured into trying to make him happy, time I wish I had back now, and I can't help feeling like I should have known from the very first beer he ever served me that he was a man who couldn't stick, like there's something wrong with my head that I didn't.

The last time I seen Benny was the day I had to tell him about

Eddie's baby. We were sitting in this empty parking lot in his daddy's Cadillac and his knuckles went white on the steering wheel and these big tears come out and mess up his shirt front, which was always pressed so nice because his mama used to work for a dry cleaners. He dropped me off in my parent's driveway after that, but even mad as he was, he hugged me real tight before I got out of that car for the last time, and right then I felt how much he must of cared for me to still have it in him to touch me after what I done.

Now, I haven't thought about any of this for years, mainly because whenever I do the memories start to come, all murky and blurred, the way I see after too much Wild Turkey. Which is what I start drinking the minute I hang up with Marge. I turn on Oprah first, then switch to Dr. Phil, who always makes me think I can fix my problems, then end up watching Jerry Springer, which usually makes me feel like my problems aren't so bad even if I can't fix them, but nothing helps. The way I feel about Benny is sudden and terrible and sad. It makes me notice the stains in my carpet and the holes in my couch and the dirty streaks high up on the windows where I can't reach and I have to go sit on the back porch and smoke until I feel better.

At least when Eddie went he left me the house. He didn't want to bother with no alimony or child support, but neither did he bother with dividing things up and that house was all we had. So I figure I'm lucky and that's where I stayed. And it's not like I got nothing to show for all those years – I got Marie and Jack, and I'm real proud of them kids, too. Not a trace of Eddie anywhere, except sometimes when Jack tips his head to the side in this particular way that reminds me of Eddie before he got it in his head he wanted to see the world. That's what he said. I don't know, sometimes I can't blame him. I wanted to see the world too, but somebody had to take care of those kids and I wasn't like Eddie. I couldn't just go.

For a while after Eddie left I'd get to feeling lonesome, but between work and grocery shopping and laundry-folding and parent-teacher conferences and doctors' appointments, it's not like I ever had much time to think about it. But sometimes after the kids were in bed and the house was quiet, it'd come over me, and I'd start thinking maybe I'd get myself a snazzy hairdo or some new clothes. I even tried dating every now and again, men I met at work or on a night I could get a babysitter and hit the Shepherd Bar with Marge, but even that didn't make me feel less lonely. Just more tired. It didn't fill up the emptiness inside me. But the truth is I felt empty even before Eddie left, so his leaving didn't affect me the way you might think.

Now the kids are gone, it sometimes feels like I'm drowning in that emptiness, or maybe like I'm already dead. Sometimes I wish I was. I have this idea that dying is like leaving all these suitcases stuffed with your unpaid bills and lonely nights at the desk of a fancy-pants hotel and riding an elevator up to a room with big windows and a king-size bed made up real pretty with white sheets and a down comforter like you see in the catalogs, and you get to sleep all night without waking up until you're good and ready, and then room service brings you Denny's Grand Slam with orange juice in a wine glass and you didn't even have to do nothing for it except answer the door. But I don't know what happens after that. Maybe you just get back in bed and wake up with the sun streaming over you morning after morning until you feel like getting up, and what you decide to do on that day is heaven. I don't know what I'd decide to do. Maybe if I weren't so tired I might be able to figure that out right now and do it.

I'm into my fifth drink when I get it in my head about Benny. The truth is I have spent more than half my life regretting what I did. And I have more than paid the price. It comes to me suddenly. I think, maybe he's divorced. Even if he's not, maybe he'll see me across the room at the reunion and know he has to leave his wife. And the more I think it, the more it seems true. I think, we'll see each other and time will stop. We will realize we are still in love. We will get the chance to go back and start over, get married, move into a two story house on High Street where all the pretty dogwoods bloom. It will be like a new beginning and Jack and Marie and his kids will be like brothers and sisters and we will have big Christmases that fill that hollowness I've been feeling all these years. But when I wake up in the morning with my head pounding and see that woman with the puffy eyes and gray streaks staring back at me in the bathroom mirror, I know for a fact what a silly idea this is. How can I expect Benny to recognize me? I can't even recognize myself. And it's not just me. The waitress at the diner, the teller at the bank – it's not that they haven't seen me before, there's just nothing to fix their eyes on when they try.

Now, I don't know what on earth possesses me to go to that reunion. I don't want to go. Still, once Marge twists me into going, I decide I will lose a pound or two, but by the time we pull into the parking lot of that high school I've gained four instead and the pink chiffon number I bought at the Dress Barn with Marge don't fit so good in the waist.

Something about the sight of the doors as we're walking up to that old high school puts me in mind of the last time I ever walked through them, the night of graduation when Randy and Ron and Lucy and Marge and me got tanked up and rode through town in the back of Sam's pickup. When Ron got hot and took his shirt off, the wind swept it out of his hand, so Randy took his shorts off and let those go too. By the time we passed McGraw's, none of us had a stitch on, so Sam hid his truck in some brush at Jumper's Hole and we went splashing into the water with the moonlight shining all around us, bobbing and laughing and diving until we had to find our way back following the trail of jeans and panties and tee-shirts like some pervert version of those fairy tale kids with the breadcrumbs. Feeling our oats, they used say, and the memory of it is so clear that I'm not sure if it's a memory or if I'm feeling it right this very second.

But as soon as we walk through those doors it suddenly hits me what a terrible idea this was. I feel kind of dizzy and my heart's pounding so hard I swear you can see it beating though all those layers of ciaffone. And wouldn't you know, right off the bat Marge spots Randy Sanders and starts in on the swooning. "My God," Marge says. "He looks exactly the same." Now this is a lie, but when I point out that Randy had a chin in high school, Marge just says, "Shut your mouth, Patty." So I do. Especially after I notice Holly Belker, who is so much thinner than she was in high school that I can feel my own belly straining against the belt of that new dress. Then I see Lucy Moore. That girl competed with me over every single thing. Outfits, cheerleading, grades – even Benny, whose eye she never caught, but I worried back then. And the first thing I notice is how much fatter she got than me, and this makes me feel great for a second, like someone else is worse off. Then she smiles like she's real glad to see me, and right away I feel mean and small. We were good friends, went to a Styx concert back in the day. Lucy's father drove us there and Lucy drank so much beer with her fake I.D. that she threw up on the way home, and her father had to stop and clean the mess off the side of his truck with the windshield wand at a gas pump. That is the first thing we talk about after twenty-five years. And it's funny how it feels like yesterday, like time is nothing, just a breeze that slips through your fingers, but we're still here, and something about that makes me feel solid for a second, like maybe time doesn't mean anything but these lines on my face and a few extra pounds.

Then Ron is there, who I haven't seen since the night of our naked parade. When we hug hello, Ron tries to pick me up the way he used to when we were young, but he's too weak and I'm too fat, so we pull away, embarassed for a second, then bust out laughing.

"Patty Rae Lapone," he says. "I didn't recognize you with your clothes on." Then we cut up again, and it feels so good to laugh. It's the first time I have in longer than I can remember, like joy I didn't even know was still in me is rushing out into the world where it's not so lonely. And before I know it, Sam is standing next to me too, and is he a sight for sore eyes. Seeing his smile again makes me remember all those days when just passing him in the hallway cheered me up after Mama and Daddy stayed up fighting until I got on the bus for school. Then he introduces me to his wife, who has a face that is nice in the exact same way Sam's is, and right away Sam asks if I still swim.

"Not for years," I say, and it's true.

"I can't believe that," Sam says now. "You was always a fish." And he is right. I was a fish. And not just in those chlorinated pools. There didn't used to be a body of water in Lake County I didn't swim. I didn't care about undertow or riptides or rapids in the Crystal River. I just wanted to be out there in that underwater coolness that always made me feel closer to what life was all about. But after the kids, even swimming got to be too much trouble and I just didn't have it in me at the end of the day. Didn't want my blow-dry to get wet, or sandy feet making sandy floormats I'd just have to clean up later. Didn't want to have to hunt around for a bathing suit that might fit me. Even one of Eddie's shirts wouldn't cover those veins and bulges from having kids, and I couldn't do like my neighbor lady growing up who wore control-top pantyhose under her bathing suit. I made fun, but now I know. Never even taught the kids to swim. They learned anyway, it's hard not to with all this water around us everywhere, but I never even took them to the beach, that's how bad I felt.

But now I look at the way Ron's shoulders have shrunk and how Lucy's cheekbones have disappeared and the little crinkles around the edges of Sam's eyes when he smiles, and I realize that I thought I was the only one got old. And Marge, of course, but seeing her over the years makes it harder to tell the difference. But for some reason I thought everybody else was still as fresh and perfect as I remember them, and here I been walking around feeling ashamed of what happens to everyone, what's natural. Half the men got no hair and everybody's features are blurrier and rounder, like we're all dissolving. Maybe that's what dying is, I think, just dissolving and dissolving until you're gone. But if that's true I'm only halfway there, something I know the minute I see Benny Goodwin looking at me from across the room. It comes to me just like that: *I'm not dead.*

But when Benny sees me looking back at him I suddenly want to look for a place to hide. I'm ashamed of every decision I ever made in my entire life, which isn't that different than the way I feel most days anyway. Because Benny looks like twenty-five years of three square meals and long nights of sleep and bills paid on time, and I feel like every cigarette and shot of Wild Turkey and Hot Fudge Ice Cream Cake at the Big Boy I ever gave into. I feel like he can tell just by looking at me that messing things up with him was the biggest mistake of my life.

"Patty Rae," he says when he walks over to me, and his voice is exactly the same. "It is good to see you."

"Benny Goodwin," I say. "It is nice to see you too." Up close he looks just the same, almost, except like he grew up some. His shirt, I notice, is still perfectly pressed.

"How have you been?" he asks.

Now, I have never been any good at hiding things. Many a cashier has got more than they bargained for when they asked me how I was. But for some reason it seems real important all of a sudden that Benny not know how bad I feel.

"Oh, fine," I say, straightening a little. "Just fine. And you?"

"Can't complain," Benny says, which is such a Benny thing to say that I have to smile at that. He always was content.

He asks where I'm living now, and all about Marie and Jack.

I ask where he lives and about his children too, since I heard he has three. He tells me he was sorry to hear about Eddie, says he heard it down to Jon's Barber Shop while he was home visiting his folks a few years back, and then we stand around making chit-chat about who we've seen so far, but something happens to Benny's face as we talk. He starts to get that exact same look that he used to get when we'd been broken up for a time and he'd start hanging around again, all shy and hopeful, like maybe if he's lucky, I'll let him back in.

It is just thrilling the way he looks at me. Like he can still see me. That is how I know I am still there. And after a while it gets real quiet around us. It gets so quiet that it seems like all there is in that great big gym is the two of us. And right there in the middle of all that silence, I do something I don't even know I'm going to do.

"Benny," I say. "I'm sorry."

Now, I did not know how much I wanted to say this, but as soon as I do, I know it is the whole reason I came to this reunion in the first place. But the words aren't even out of my mouth when a woman walks up and the noise rushes around us again like nothing happened at all, and so fast that I start to think maybe nothing did. Then Benny is introducing me to his wife.

Benny's wife seems so happy to meet me that right away I start to feel guilty that I been having all these thoughts about Benny for weeks now, like if I look her in the eye she'll see my plans to make off with her husband plain as day. But when I do there's nothing but kindness there and suddenly I feel so glad for Benny, having a nice wife like that. And I feel something lift inside me, a weight I been carrying around ever since that day I had to tell Benny about the baby, because you can tell just from looking at his wife that she's the type who wouldn't run off and sleep with no bartender. Like she knows the value of what she's got and won't screw it up. This is what I know about her before Benny has even finished introducing us.

Benny's wife looks real young, but Benny says no, just a year younger than us. Graduated from Senath High the year after we did. The salutatorian, he brags, and you can just see how proud he is. Then Benny starts bragging to her about me, how one time I swam all the way across Clearwater Cove on a dare. And it really knocks me out that first of all, I done something like that, because Clearwater Cove is a mile of cold water, couldn't get my body across it now if I tried, is what I think, and second, that he remembers it. But the fact that he does reminds me a little of the girl I used to be. Bold, that was Patty Rae Lapone. Not afraid to do something foolish just for fun. Then Benny's wife says their daughter Missy swims too, and gets out her wallet and starts showing me pictures, but it's like I can't really hear what she's saying because all of the sudden I can feel the wind on my face and the water around me, and it's like my body remembers that swim even if my mind can't quite get me in the middle of that cove anymore.

But then Barry Lippert and Chuck Rayburn walk up and clap Benny on the back and start jawing about the old football team playing in the state championship game senior year, and I know my time with Benny is over. I drift away then and head off to check on Marge, who has not left Randy Sanders' side since we arrived, and when Randy sees me, he greets me so friendly that I get to feeling real bad about that crack I made about his chin. But all the time we are talking, I can't help but wonder if Benny even heard what I said. I think, maybe he thought I was about to ask him to speak up, or excuse myself to the ladies' room. Maybe he doesn't know what I meant. Then I look over to where Benny is standing with his nice wife and those two old football buddies and think, well, it probably don't matter much to him anyhow. He probably hasn't thought of any of that in years. Losing me probably doesn't seem like the point after which everything changed for him, the way losing him does for me. He was always gonna be somebody. But it matters so much to me that he heard what I said. And I know I won't get another chance, even if I do talk to him. I know I won't have the nerve to say it again.

Then everyone is eating little pigs-in-a-blanket and cheese toasts from the buffet table and the DJ starts playing songs from back in high school, and Marge and Randy dance to "Lost in Love" and Betty Filmore starts dancing to "Maniac" in this way that says she's had too much sauce, and pretty soon half the old cheerleading squad is on that dance floor too, still holding their drinks in their hands, dancing to "My Sharona" and "Celebration" and doing the moves to "Y.M.C.A" until Stacy Peters breaks her wine glass all over the floor and the waiters come out to clean up the mess. But by the time all the pieces are swept up and the floor is dry, the mood is kind of broken, and the next thing you know the DJ puts on "Last Dance" and then we're all drifting toward the door and out into the parking lot, and just like that our reunion is over.

Well, I hug Sam and Lucy and them, and we all promise to meet up down to McGraw's one day, and it sure has been great to see everybody. But this whole time I am saying my goodbyes I am also looking for Benny. And when the crowd finally thins out, I see him walking toward me. Then he is standing in front of me. "Patty," he says when he leans in to hug me, "It's okay. You were just a kid." He pats my back and holds me for a long time, like I'm a child he's trying to soothe. "I forgave you a long time ago," he says. Then he pulls back and smiles right into my eyes, and I am filled with the feeling that I have fixed something I did not know could ever be fixed. In that moment it feels like all of life is there between us, the sadness and loss and regret, and somehow it is okay. It is better than okay, even. It is what I have wanted to feel between Benny and me for so long, and I feel truly good for the first time in twenty-five years just standing there with him. It is a real comfort just having him near again after all these years.

Then Marge says she's leaving with Randy Sanders and don't wait up, and Sam toots the horn of his pickup on his way out, and

Benny leaves with his wife in their station wagon, waving as he pulls away just like he always did. I sit in my car for a long time after that, roll down the windows and smoke a cigarette and fiddle with the radio until I find some oldies for the drive home, and wouldn't you know it, I'm the last car to leave.

I swing out onto High Street and pass Benny's old house, then McGraw's a few blocks up, but just as I'm about to pull onto the highway I see the turnoff for Clearwater Cove, and the next thing I know I've turned down that gravel two-track instead. I can smell that mossy lake smell and feel the breeze off the water and see the moon shining on the surface, which is so glassy and calm that the light makes a path that leads right to me, so I get out of the car and kick off my pumps, and pretty soon my dress and bra and pantyhose are in a heap on the shore, but I feel so light it's like I've left twenty-five years somewhere in that pile too. Then the water is around my ankles and I'm walking into that path of moonlight, so bright I can see my own reflection just before I break the water and start to swim.

The Marionette Theater

They had arrived in Prague in the middle of a rainstorm, the water pooling in gutters that ran down the center of the streets and prevented puddles as they rolled their wheeled suitcases over the cobblestones of Sokolovska to the apartment where Jonathan stayed on business trips, and to which he had returned each afternoon from his meetings to whisk Josie off on a tour of the castle, or a walk over the Charles Bridge, or a lecture on the history of the Jewish Cemetery. It was not their honeymoon – a cruise to Barbados that would leave port the day after the wedding—but Josie's friends kept calling it one anyway. "The *first* honeymoon," they said, and when Jonathan overheard them, he flashed the women a smile. "We're so happy," he told them, "we need two!"

And now they were here, and the city was every bit as beautiful as Jonathan had promised it would be, if not more so, in the slanting August light. But as they strolled along the cobblestones of the Golden Lane, stood in the tiny house where Kafka had written *The Metamorphosis*, took an evening cruise down the Voltava sipping champagne from slender crystal flutes, Josie could not shake the feeling that none of it was real. The castle looked like the one she had seen at Disney World, the Charles Bridge as if it were built of styrafoam bricks, the exterior of St. Vitus like a façade supported by scaffolding, so that when they had walked inside, the organ pipes and pulpits had surprised her.

It was a feeling that had dogged her long before their arrival in Prague. Ever since Jonathan had pulled the diamond ring from his pocket and slipped it in on her finger in the horse-drawn carriage he'd hired to take them around the park at Christmastime, nothing had seemed real. The ring itself was so bright and golden it could have dropped from a gumball machine, and when Jonathan said, "Will you marry me?" his words did not seem to come from deep inside him, as Josie felt a question like that should. And then there were the wedding preparations: cakes that looked like sculptures, flowers so perfect she had to touch them to know they weren't silk, wedding gowns so white they looked almost blue. And the showers: Josie sat amidst grinning women who stroked her arms as if in welcome to the world of mixmasters and food processors and something called "the clean up factor" but as she unwrapped each new blender or microwave or toaster oven, they felt as flimsy as the cardboard kitchen set she'd had as a child, which had disintigrated into pulpy lumps when the basement had flooded.

Tonight they had tickets for the National Marionette Theater, the event Jonathan had saved for their last night in Prague, and as they ordered plates of goulash under the awning of a café in Old Town before heading to the theater, Josie thought back to their first date when he'd described it all to her—the performance of Mozart's *Don Giovanni*, the black-cloaked puppeteers that made the darkness behind the set seem more alive than the puppets themselves, the way the tradition stretched back for centuries. "And the puppets," he'd said, reaching for her hand across the table of the trendy bar where he'd taken her that first night. "You will love the puppets." But in truth it had never been his description of their painted faces, or their elaborate costumes, or the crowds that packed the theater to see them each night that convinced her that she would. It was the way he had said *will*, as if this was already their future together, because she was thirty-one years old and tired of the men her parents kept inviting over on the Sundays she joined them for dinner at their house in Gladstone. "A Chiefs fan," her father would say by way of explaining why a young man from the gun club or the son of one of the Elks was joining them, and to prove this wasn't a set-up, Josie's father would hand him a beer and lead him downstairs to watch the game.

And now she was in Prague with Jonathan just as he'd promised she would be on that very first date, but even Jonathan did not seem real to her, hadn't seemed real since the moment he'd reclined in the carriage after proposing and began rehearsing all the things he'd soon be saying. "I'd like you to meet *my wife*," he tried. Or: "*My wife* always says . . ." Then: "I was just telling *my wife*." It was supposed to be a joke, but Josie had the feeling he wasn't telling it to her, and she'd felt a sudden hollowness in her stomach then that hadn't gone away. But ever since they'd called their parents from a pay phone at the west end of the park she hadn't had time to think about that hollowness because there were invitations to order and venues to reserve and the registry to fill out, and then the engagement party Aunt Mildred had planned and that family reunion of Jonathan's they'd promised to attend in Vermont, and now the wedding was only three weeks away and Josie knew she did not want to marry him.

For a week she had been trying to tell him. They would arrive at the apartment after a concert in St. George's, or find themselves alone in the Palace Gardens, or pause to inspect a set of vases in the window of a shop in Wenceslaus Square, and there would be a lull in all their forward motion, an opening, and she'd turn to him to say *look* or *listen* or *we need to talk*. But whenever she tried to speak, her mouth would not form the words. And now the week was over and they were leaving Prague in the morning, and as soon as the plane touched down in Kansas City there would be the response cards to count and the seating charts to arrange and the second alteration with the shop girls who wanted her gown to be more fitted, though she could not breathe in the thing as it was, and before she knew it they'd be on that cruise to Barbados, the wedding already behind them.

Now she faced Jonathan across the table, watching him lift spoonfuls of soup to his mouth. She stared at him so long that he paused, his spoon in midair.

"Is something wrong?" he asked.

She did not know what would happen afterward. She could not picture his expression, nor the shock of their parents and neighbors and friends, nor the magnitude of the plans that would have to be undone. She only knew she had to tell him the truth.

But she heard herself answer, as if from a distance: "Nothing, darling."

"Are you sure?" he asked. "You look pale."

"I'm fine," she said.

They were words that did not come from inside her. They came from somewhere else instead, and they satisfied Jonathan, who turned back to his soup, nodded at a passing waiter, smiled when the Orloj in the square behind them began ringing out seven o'clock. But with each clang Josie felt herself growing numb, and by the time the waitress delivered their goulash, she realized she could not feel her limbs. Then Jonathan paid the bill, and Josie felt herself being steered through the narrow streets to a tiny theater at the top of a cramped staircase that smelled of the Voltava. There was a moment before they entered when she might have spoken, and another when Jonathan paused to adjust his tie, and another after they were ushered down the aisle just before the show began. But by then it was too late. The doors had closed and the curtain had lifted and the puppets were already clattering away, whirling through the dance they'd been performing for centuries.

The Score

'm already pulling a sheet of cookies out of the oven by the time Mike's Blazer comes snaking up the driveway. Jimmy and I arrived first and let ourselves in with the key under the welcome mat, started the fire and shoveled the snow drifts that stopped his Escort at the mailbox, but now we watch through the kitchen window as Mike parks under the basketball hoop and Ricky, Lance and Dave pile out with a slender girl whose blue-black hair shines in the late afternoon sunlight.

"Who's that?" I say.

"Some girl from their building," Jimmy says as he heads out to greet them, and I'm transferring the cookies onto a cooling rack when Mike walks into the kitchen and says, "Wow."

"Chocolate chip," I say.

"My favorite," he tells me, and I pretend I didn't know.

Mike is tall and broad with spiky blond hair and a spray of pale freckles across his nose, and he wraps his arms around my shoulders from behind me, vice-like, and lifts me right off the floor. "When am I going to find a nice girl like you?" he breathes in my ear, and I swat him away with the spatula, even though this means more to me than anything Jimmy ever says to me, and it's the main reason I'm here in the first place.

These weekends at Mike's family cabin are when I'm most happy, when I'm surrounded by men whose meals I've cooked, whose hangovers I've nursed, whose button-downs I've pressed over the four years I've known them, men who tell Jimmy that he better treat me right, that a girl like me doesn't come along every day, that one day I'll make a great wife. But when I walk into the living room, I can tell right away that something is different by the jitter in Lance's eyes, the drum of Ricky's fingers, the fever in Dave's voice when he says to me, "Angela, this is Tara."

The girl is even prettier up close, flawless ivory skin and wide green eyes, but it's more than just that: she's *sexy*. It's the pink pumps that peek out beneath her skintight jeans, the red nails on the hand she extends to me, the smoke I can hear in her *hello*.

"It's nice to meet you," I say, but I'm lying, which for some reason always makes me sound especially sincere.

Most weekends at Mike's cabin are just to escape – term papers and exams in the old days, cubicles and deadlines now that graduation has turned us loose in the world. But this weekend, Mike has a purpose in bringing us together: an experiment he's doing for his job in sports medicine. After a couple rounds of Euchre and the lasagne I make for supper, he drags three coolers into the living room and sets a box with a light and a button on the coffee table. When the light blinks, he tells us, we slap our hand on the button, and a digital screen measures our speed. After every beer, we record our time on the chart he's taped to the table, and the person with the fastest average score by the end of the night wins.

"Drink, blink, slap," Mike tells us. "Got it?"

The game begins. Mike hands out the first beer, and everyone lounges around the fire, talking about the morning Mike's father asked Jimmy to help skin the moose whose head now hangs over the mantel and the night Mike's mother backed her Impala over my suitcases, inside stories I can joke about while the guys crack up, and things seem so normal that I start to relax. But by the second beer, we've moved on to drinking stories – how Ricky drove a stranger's car home from the bar once and Lance almost burned his parents' house to the ground – and it's then that Tara tells one of her own, about an old man who let her sleep in his spare room when she couldn't find her way home one night in college, then tried to feel her up. She's leaning forward as she tells it, giving us a glimpse of what the old man was trying to feel, and it's not the laughter that follows, but the pitch and volume of it, that tells me I'm fading into the whitewashed logs.

After Mike passes around the third beer, Jimmy's bottle explodes when he opens it, so I get up to find some paper towels, but by the time I return from the kitchen, Tara is somehow in Ricky's lap, and when I look over again a few minutes later, his hands are splayed over her hips. But by the fourth beer she's on her feet again, dancing to the radio she's turned up while Dave grinds his pelvis into her back, and when Marky Mark yells *feel it feel it* Lance moves in from the front, making a Tara sandwich.

It's not until the fifth beer that I notice how hard I'm clenching my teeth, and the sixth before I realize I've got a full-blown headache, so after searching the bathroom for some aspirin I head into the kitchen to check there instead, but when I turn on the light, I find Tara in a corner with Ricky, holding his seventh bottle out of reach. "Woes Wicky want a Wudwiser?" she asks, and though I've never seen him baby talk with any of the women he's called girlfriends, *Wicky* says "Wes."

But by the eighth beer, Tara looks bored. After we've all recorded our scores on the chart, she picks up her ninth and walks over to where Mike is reclined on a wingback.

"How come *you're* such a stiff?" she asks, ruffling the hair I've been dying to run my fingers through for four years like it's a right she's earned in just four hours.

"A stiff?" he says.

"Loosen up," she tells him. "*Do* something."

"Like what?" he asks, so she removes one of the pink pumps from her feet, pours his beer into it, and hands it to him. When he drinks it without stopping, she smiles, tosses her hair back, and says, "I bet I can top that."

I'm thrilled when Mike looks unimpressed.

"Then top it," he shrugs.

Tara keeps her eyes on Mike as she reaches down and takes off her other shoe. Then she reaches up and slips off her earrings and her watch. She peels off her sweater, then slides out of her jeans. When she unhooks her bra and steps out of her panties, she walks over to the back door leading down to the lake and says, "I'm going for a swim."

For a second, no one moves. Then they're up, howling and hopping in a storm of tee shirts and boxer shorts, tearing out into the snow after her. By the time even Jimmy goes out on the deck to watch, I'm shaking so hard that I have to sit down, even though I don't care what Jimmy does anymore and have been meaning to break up with him for years, but how do you say *I don't love you anymore* and still seem nice?

When they return from the lake, icicles have formed on their hair. They put their clothes on as quickly as they came off and huddle around the fire until their teeth stop chattering, but after their naked plunge it seems like there's nothing left to top, and when Lance and Dave pass out on the bunks in Mike's room and Ricky sacks out on the couch, I head off to the bathroom to get ready for bed. In the mirror that hangs above the sink, I flash myself the kind of smile Tara gave Mike right before she took her clothes off, give my hair a toss, say to my reflection, *I bet I can top that*, but the words sound hollow coming out my mouth, like they do when I'm interviewing for a job I already know I'm not going to get.

I feel a little better after I've washed my face and brushed my teeth, but on my way back to the bedroom where Jimmy and I sleep I have to pass through the living room, and that's when I see Mike. He's sprawled under the flap of a sleeping bag with Tara, on top of her, moving over her, and I slam our bedroom door to keep out the sounds they make in the night, the cries that lift and crest, then fall and rise, the single shout that pierces the frozen dark.

In the morning, they drift into the kitchen one by one, drink the coffee I've brewed, eat the pancakes I make. Mike asks me if I'm married when I set down his plate, and Dave says I'm a keeper when he takes his first bite, but when I turn back to the griddle they whisper the words they think are too crude for my ears: *easy*, they say, *begging for it, slut*, and when I hear their muffled laughter I look up and see Tara, awake now, crouched in the living room by herself. Five minutes pass, then ten, but none of them will look at her, and no one invites her to join us.

I always wait until after I've served them all to fix myself a plate, but this morning, I fix two, and instead of squeezing around the table, I walk out to where Tara shivers on the couch. When I sit down beside her and hand her a plate, she looks up shyly and says, "Thanks." She's reading the scores on Mike's chart, running her finger down the rows until she finds her own name.

She says, "I didn't win."

I say, "I didn't either."

Divining Venus

The ouija board in Venus Lockhart's basement knows lots of things. Such as: Every single boy in our sixth grade class is in love with Venus. And: In six years Venus will be the homecoming queen of our high school. Also: Venus will be Miss Isabella County one day, which isn't that surprising since she's practically a celebrity already at Immaculate Heart Elementary School. I mean, it took me years just to get a seat at that girl's lunch table, but now she lets me sit right next to her whenever I want. I get to eat her extra Twinkie and spot her sit-ups in gym class and walk home from school with her every single day. And only *I* get to play with Venus's ouija board. Not Jennie Millgate *or* Tanya Hanks, who have been in a dead heat with me for Venus's attention ever since she moved to Michigan in second grade.

Every day after school we put that ouija board between us and touch our fingertips to the indicator, then ask about all the mysteries of the universe, like why Rita Lambert got boobs before all the other girls in our class. When the spirits know the truth they will use our fingers to spell it out, like when Venus asks who will be her next boyfriend and the spirits say H-U-E-Y P-A-R-K-E-R (who she's liked for weeks).

Sister Gerald Vincent says diviners are witches, but life sure is easier when you can get all the answers, even if some questions I want to ask are against regulations, like when will I die and where is the gold buried, and others just wouldn't be polite, like why Venus has silky blonde hair and perfect skin and Calvin Klein jeans that fit her just right, but I'm stuck with red frizz and freckles and plain old Wranglers from the Quality Farm and Fleet. Or why Venus has eyes so blue they are almost purple but mine are just a shade my mother calls *hazel,* meaning they aren't really any color at all, and which anyway only reminds me of my Aunt Hazel who wears horn-rimmed glasses and eats all the garnishes off the hors d'oeuvre platters at family Christmas parties. Venus's feet are tiny too – size six – which is probably the thing I am most jealous about since mine are size nine-and-a-half. When my mother took my little sister Janie and me to the Back to School Sales in August, the man at Buster Brown said I looked like a large-breed puppy in my new tennis shoes. He said, "That girl is all feet."

All feet is not a very cool thing to be in the sixth grade and probably explains why the ouija board never says any boys are in love with me. Which is obvious since Teddy Schwab never asks me to play Spoons anymore, and Willie Montrose moves to another seat when I sit next to him on the bus, and Cletus DeLucca acts like he doesn't even know who I am ever since we played Mary and Joseph in the Christmas play and he put his arm around me behind the manger, which seemed all wrong for the Blessed Mother. I said, "Cletus, if you do not get your hands off me *this instant* I will scream" (all while trying to look holy, which was not the easiest thing to do). But Venus says Cletus is cute and wants to *go* with him, which means I don't know what because nobody in our class goes anywhere except out to recess.

(The only boy I'd go anywhere with is Kyle Kellerman, who sits next to me in Sister Gerald Vincent's class. Kyle already knows every single element on the periodic table by heart and also gets *3-2-1 Contact* just like I do, which we discuss every month. Sometimes he passes me notes with jokes in them, like *What kind of music does Jupiter like? Neptunes* and *How did the rocket lose his job? He was fired.* But Venus says, "Laugh at anymore of those stupid jokes, Sophie Williams, and you will be left out in the cold." Venus says so much as looking in Kyle Kellerman's direction could make me unpopular, but I can't seem to help myself. I just love all that science talk.)

Here is another thing I can't ask that ouija board: why *I* can't have parents just like Venus's who drive a Volkswagen van and keep pet rabbits in the back yard and named *me* after the Goddess of Love and Beauty, who is the whole reason Venus's parents found each other and fell in love. And let me tell you, Venus's parents are more in love than any people I have ever seen except on television. Venus's mother walks around in her nightgown and her father has a ponytail and they went to this concert called Woodstock one time, and whenever Venus's father starts playing his guitar, he will walk all over that house until he finds her mother, who will swing a towel over her head in time to *Foxy Lady*, or use a hairbrush as a microphone, and I just can't help but feel a little dizzy every time I get around all that romance. I can't help worrying that my parents are headed straight for divorce because instead of singing to my mother and playing the guitar, my father reads off the prices of duck decoys from Cabela's while my mother washes the dishes and says, "Uh-huh."

When you have parents like Venus's, you can turn Rick Springfield all the way up and crank call your friends and watch game shows until *Phil Donahue* comes on, and if you forget to take off your shoes at the door you never have to worry about giving someone a migraine. Plus you never have to go to the doctor, because whenever Venus gets sick her mother just puts a little vodka in her orange juice and lets her stay home from school. My father would call that irresponsible, but parents like Venus's are just more concerned with the important things which they teach you early so you never say dumb things like I did last week when Venus's father showed us this chunk of stone he chipped off the building where

John Lennon was shot. When I said, "Who's John Lennon?" Venus turned to her father and said, "Larry, I want to apologize on behalf of my friend. They do not have MTV at her house."

Venus calls her parents *Larry* and *Charlene* instead of *Mom* and *Dad* like everybody else I know. They also told me to call them *Larry* and *Charlene* and for a while I tried to act like it wasn't a big deal for me to call adults by their first names. I practiced in front of the mirror: "How's it going, Charlene?" "See you later, Larry." I was getting pretty good at it until Venus stayed over at my house one night and called my father *John* at the dinner table. Well, my father started ranting to my mother about manners plain and simple and his students at the college who don't take off their ball caps. He said, "I don't know about you, Mrs. Williams, but I could do without this first-name-basis-what-all." So now I'm back to calling Venus's parents *Mr. and Mrs. Lockhart*, which feels more normal to me anyway and doesn't bother them a bit. They are just as happy to see me whenever I walk through their door, and never get mad if I drop food on the floor or spill my Coke by accident.

With Venus as my best friend, no one dares make fun of my Tupperware lunchbox or pick me last for kickball, and I never have to eat with Carrie MacIntosh, who wears this big ugly strap that holds her glasses in place and tells all these lies about being related to the Princess of Wales. Everything in sixth grade starts going along just perfect, and I couldn't be happier.

Then Sister Gerald Vincent says it is Reverence for Life and Family Day for all sixth graders at Immaculate Heart, and sends the boys to the gym so she can talk to us about Becoming a Person. She says, "You will all be young ladies soon. You will need to know the facts of life." Now *The Facts of Life* is one of the only television programs I am allowed to watch, but the movie Sister Gerald shows starts off with flowers and bees and birds and eggs, and we all sit around passing notes and rolling our eyes because if we wanted *Mutual of Omaha's Wild Kingdom* we'd just go home and watch it. Then out of nowhere it switches to these outlines of men and women with a bunch of organs drawn over their crotches, and it gets so quiet that I can hear Carrie MacIntosh sucking on her inhaler all the way across the room. I can hear the clock tick, and the wind outside, and even my own heart, which starts racing like crazy.

And when the lights go up, that whole classroom just goes wild. Mimi Carter wants to know will you have a baby if you use the same toilet as a boy, and Wanda Wiggins asks if it will happen if you sit next to one on the bus, and Little-Miss-Know-It-All Jennie Millgate says her sister had a baby after sitting in the back seat of a car with a boy so why should it be any different on the bus? Sister Gerald says you cannot get pregnant from any of these things directly, but that we must be very careful not to put ourselves on the path to temptation which is why the back seats of cars are a bad idea in general, and while we're on the subject, the bus seats, too. She says we must always think of the Virgin Mary, our model of chastity, and if that doesn't work, then those starving children with flies on their faces in the ads with Sally Struthers.

Well, I am so relieved to know that Willie Montrose has only been afraid to sit with me on the bus because he is looking out for my own best interest that I try to smile at him after school to let him know that I'm not mad about it, but he just glares at me and looks the other way. Then Venus starts singing *Sophie and Willie sitting in a tree, K-I-S-S-I-N-G!*

Now, normally I would *never* contradict Venus about anything, but I cannot just stand by and keep quiet about this. I have to set that girl straight. I say, "I do *not* like Willie Montrose. I'm just glad to know why he doesn't sit with me on the bus."

And that's where all the trouble starts.

Venus grabs me so hard I can feel her fingernails dig into my arm. She pushes me right off the sidewalk. She says, "You listen to me, Sophie Williams. Only people who are married can have babies."

I say, "Sister Gerald said . . ."

But Venus cuts me off. "What does that stupid old nun know? Nuns can't have babies, either."

When I ask why not, Venus looks at me like she can't believe she's stuck hanging out with the most ignorant person on the planet.

"Because they're *not married*," she says. And suddenly her face is all red and pinched up and I think maybe she's going to cry. She gives me a little shake. "Do you hear me?" she asks. Then she shoves me away and storms off. Well, I chase right after her, but the whole time I'm worried that if I don't fix this, she'll figure out how boring I am and not let me come over after school anymore, so I get busy trying to think up ways to prove that I still deserve to be her friend. I'm so busy deciding on the best way to impress her I don't even notice that we're walking toward Bond Street, which is the only street in all of Middleton that I'm not allowed to cross, but when I ask Venus why we're not going to her house like always, she just says, "Let's go to Island Park."

I say, "I'm not supposed to cross Bond Street." But as soon as I say it I wish I could take it back because Venus turns those big purple eyes on me and I start to worry that she can see right down to the part of me that is so scared of my parents and Sister Gerald and Kyle Kellerman and the whole wide world that she'd dump me right away if she knew the truth.

She says, "You are such a baby. You do whatever your parents say." And just the way she says it tells me how soon I'll be eating my lunch with Carrie MacIntosh.

So when the light changes, I run as fast as I can across Bond Street. I balance on the guardrail of the bridge and hang upside down off the monkey bars and go headfirst down the tallest slide in the park just to make sure Venus knows I don't care *what* my parents say. Then we get on the swings and pump our legs back and forth until we're flying, until I'm up in the sky next to Venus, until we are higher than anything in our whole town and nothing on earth can stop us.

Crossing Bond Street gets me three weeks of coming straight home after school without telephone privileges. I might have gotten away with it if Venus ever wanted to go home, but for a whole week we walked to Island Park after school and stayed there until it was time for my mother to pick me up. Then our neighbor Melvin Blackwell mentioned seeing me there while he was fishing, so now I only get to talk to Venus at recess, which is no fun since Jenny Millgate and Tanya Hanks never let me get a word in edgewise. They have been just waiting for this opportunity to steal Venus away from me and I'm so afraid that by the time it's over Venus will have replaced me, even though I'm still mad at her for making me cross that street. When I said this to my mother, she said no one can *make* you do anything and I said, well if that's true then she couldn't *make* me come home after school either, and she said anymore lip out of me and I'd get grounded for another week.

And let me tell you, even though my parents fight about everything from where to set the thermostat to why my father always has to mention what a good cook his cousin Lulu is right after my mother has just fixed dinner, if there is one thing they agree on, it is how long to ground me, and for what. Hiding broccoli under my cushion at supper gets me two days, being fresh with teachers gets me one week, and earning low marks in Self Control and Work Habits gets me ten days. My parents say it hurts them more than it hurts me, but it's hard to believe when I can hear them downstairs after they've sent me to bed, eating popcorn and watching *Dallas*.

(Venus never gets grounded, and believe me, it is *not* because that girl does not know how to shake things up. Sometimes class will be going along all normal and quiet when out of the blue Venus will chirp like a bird until Sister Gerald starts lifting table skirts and opening cupboards to look for one, or she'll throw a wet wad of toilet paper up on the ceiling and let it drip until it leaves a little puddle on the floor. Then she will raise her hand and say, "Sister, I believe someone has had an accident." Well, all the people sitting around that puddle jump right up and start looking around at each other and down at their pants, but whenever our principal calls Venus's house to complain, Charlene just thanks Father Donald and tells him that he needs to get a life.)

Anyway, at first being grounded isn't so bad since my sister Janie knows how to use our new remote control to switch from *The Waltons* to *Days of Our Lives* when my parents aren't looking. Then Stefano Di Mera's hired assassin tries to break up Roman Brady's wedding to Marlena Evans, and Janie and I get so caught up that we don't even notice my father standing right behind us. Well, the very next day he comes home from work and reads us this book called "Where Did I Come From?" that is like the movie Sister Gerald showed on Reverence for Life and Family Day. Then he wants to discuss it, so I ask if you have to be married to have a baby, but my father just says I sure as hell better be. Then my mother wants to know was that really necessary, but my father says it was because God only knows what we've picked up watching soaps. So now it's back to *The Waltons*, which kind of drags after all that daytime drama, so Janie and I sometimes settle for one of those PBS shows about Mt. Everest or the Great Wall of China, and I just sit there wishing I could move someplace far away like that, where I can cross any street I want and be in love with Kyle Kellerman and never have to listen to my father talk about fallopian tubes again.

Well, I nearly dry up and blow away waiting for those three weeks to be over, but just about the time they are, my parents up and take us on a spring break trip to Washington, D.C.. My father says it's important for Janie and me to see other parts of the country so we don't end up breast-feeding babies on our front porches all day and thinking that's all there is in life, so we go see the pandas, and a museum with Fonzie's jacket from *Happy Days* and the ruby slippers from *The Wizard of Oz*. We even take a detour through Virginia Beach where my parents used to live, and they point out the tennis club where they first met and the restaurant where my father proposed, and I try to picture it all as they talk but it's hard to imagine a time when they weren't making a federal case over who takes out the trash or whether my father's relatives can drop by whenever they damn well please.

A week later I hop off the bus all set for my life to go back to normal, but when I open up the front door to school I see something that stops me cold. Right there in the hallway, sitting on a bench, are Kyle Kellerman and Venus Lockhart. Talking! Kyle is waving his hands like he's explaining something and Venus is tossing all that shiny hair around, and for a second I can't breathe. I can't say a word. I just stand there with my poncho dripping rain all over the floor, because Venus is the one who is always telling *me* to stay away from him.

Then it hits me: Venus likes Kyle Kellerman too!

It also hits me that if Kyle figures out he can have Venus for his girlfriend, he will never speak to me again, and it is just amazing how I go from liking Venus to hating her all in the same second. But right then Kyle sees me and says, "Hi Sophie." Well, I march right past like I've never seen either of them in my entire life, but before I even get to my locker I regret it since I am nothing without Venus. I try to be extra nice to her at lunch and even share part of my peanut butter sandwich with her, but when I get permission to use the bathroom, I go straight to her locker and stick my ice cream cone into her hat.

All week long I ride the bus home after school and dream up more ways to get back at Venus, like turning her rabbits loose and filling up her shampoo bottle with the hair remover my mother puts on her legs. But I get so bored by the end of the week that I almost forget how mad I still am about Kyle Kellerman when she calls me up on Saturday morning and asks if I can come over. My mother drops me off at her house on her way to run errands in town, but when I walk in, I don't see Venus or Larry or Charlene anywhere. The only person in sight is a pretty girl I've never seen before watching *Charlie's Angels.*

"I'm Tiffany," the girl says, all *la-di-da,* then turns back to the television. She's about the age of my father's students at the college who sometimes babysit for Janie and me, and looks so at home that I feel out of place (though I practically live here when I'm not grounded). Well, I head off down the hall to find Venus, but when I do she's sitting on her bed with her arms wrapped around her knees looking like she's really eleven – like I am – instead of older, the way she always seems to be. Just the way her face looks makes me feel so awful about her hat that I almost apologize right off the bat, but instead I say I didn't know she had a sister, and she says, "I don't."

I say, "Who's Tiffany?"

Venus says, "She's Larry's girlfriend."

I say, "Larry has a girlfriend?"

Venus shoots me a look that says *don't ask any of your stupid questions,* so I stop right there. But I have about a million: How can Larry have a girlfriend if he has a wife? Isn't he in love with Charlene? Does my father have a girlfriend too?

When my mother comes back to pick me up, Charlene meets her in the driveway, then tells Venus to pack a bag because she's staying at my house tonight. We ride in the back seat of our Chevy Impala between sacks of groceries, and Venus rests her head against the door and looks out the window as we drive. She doesn't say a word, and I don't either, even though my head is just buzzing with things to ask. After supper, Venus helps me clear the dishes and wipe the table, then we head straight for the television. My mother reminds us: *Bedtime is at nine o'clock.* I roll my eyes at Venus to make sure she knows how much I hate my parents, but she just looks up and says in this voice I've never heard before, "Thank you, Mrs. Williams."

Well, I don't know what to make of this, but I get plenty of time to think it over because a week later it's like my parents have a new daughter. It's: "Why don't you stay another night, Venus?" and "What would Venus like for supper?" and "Why doesn't Venus take that last snickerdoodle?" and *Venus Venus Venus* all the time until I am sorry she ever moved to Michigan. Venus always says I have the most impossible parents in our whole town, but now she rides in the front seat of the Impala between them while Janie and I ride in the back. I say, "I beat everyone at Grammar Jeopardy today," or, "Sister Gerald says I did the best on my book report." But my parents only say *that's nice* and go right back to worrying about guess who. And Venus just sits there looking like a little angel the whole time, like she never stole Sister Maurice Conner's chalk last year or flushed Mary Ann Ambrose's mitten down the toilet in third grade, which is the whole reason I started worshipping her in the first place. I swear I don't even know who that girl is anymore, the way she's acting, all *please* and *thank you* and *that was delicious Mrs. Williams* until I just want to smack her.

My mother says I should be nicer to Venus because she's going through a hard time right now, but I can't help being mad about crossing Bond Street just to impress Venus now that she wants to be Miss Perfect Who Never Does Anything Wrong. I can't help feeling jealous of all the attention she's getting. It's like the rules

of the world have changed, and if I don't watch out, pretty soon
Venus will be falling asleep to my mother's backrubs and waking
up to my father's pancakes, and I'll be sharing a bed with a bunch
of orphans and living off government cheese.

It turns out that you *don't* have to be married to have a baby after
all. Tiffany is having one even though Larry is still married to
Charlene, but only until they sign some papers that say it's all over
with. But even though I am glad to know that Venus does not know
every little thing, I still keep on hoping that Larry will come back
because that house sure feels empty without him, and it's not just
because half the furniture is gone. The bean bags Charlene buys to
fill in the holes don't change how quiet it is, except when Charlene's
friends sit around in them, smoking cigarettes and talking about
Tiffany. (For weeks I have been begging Venus to tell me what a
slut is, but she just says, "If you would ever shut your mouth for five
seconds, one day I *might*.")

Then one afternoon the Volkswagen van is parked in the
driveway and Larry is on the porch talking to Charlene, and for
a second it looks like everything is back to the way it used to be.
Larry even says hello when we walk up after school, like nothing is
different, but when he tries to hug Venus she ducks under his arm
and runs inside, and Charlene just says, "I think it's going to take
her a while." Well, I follow Venus and we flop down in the bean
bags and watch the end of *Wheel of Fortune*, but out on the porch
Larry goes on about the warm weather and the daffodils in the
front flower bed, and even though I can't make out all the words, it
mostly sounds like he doesn't want to leave.

When he's gone, Venus and I head down to the basement and
pull out the ouija board. Venus asks who will win the stereo they're
giving away down at Spencer Drugs, and the spirits say V-E-N-U-S,

then I ask if Larry and Charlene will get back together like in *The Parent Trap*, but Venus pushes the board away and says, "Sophie, when are you going to stop being such a little dork?" But I know for a fact that there are ways to save your marriage because my sister Janie found this magazine at the doctor's office that explained them all. She read them out loud in the waiting room: *Bake his favorite kind of pie* and *Write sexy notes in lipstick on the bathroom mirror.* I didn't get to hear them all because when she read *Show up at his office wearing nothing but a winter coat*, my mother grabbed the magazine and threw it back on the coffee table. But Venus says it's too late for all that now that Tiffany is having a baby.

The thing is, I don't really understand why. Just because Larry is having a baby with Tiffany doesn't mean he doesn't still love Charlene. I mean, the book my father read to Janie and me said that making a baby felt like scratching an itch, only a lot nicer, but I got poison ivy after Sister Gerald took us on a field trip in the fall and I still felt the same way about Kyle Kellerman once it was over. When we go upstairs later I ask Charlene about this, but she just says it's hard to explain.

She says, "I think Larry has poison ivy too."

On the last day of sixth grade, Sister Gerald throws a corndog-and-potato-salad picnic on the lawn of the parish hall, and Kyle Kellerman writes in my memory book: "To Sophie, a cool girl I really like a lot. See you in seventh grade science!" I think, *Kyle Kellerman thinks I'm cool? Kyle Kellerman likes me a lot?* All day long I keep opening up that page just to read it again, and every time I do I forget all about my frizzy hair and freckles.

When the bell rings, Venus and I walk to her house and grab Cokes out of the refrigerator and change into shorts, and all those months stretched out in front of us without any homework feel so good. Then we go down to the basement and put the ouija board between us and the indicator says YES when Venus asks if she will win Outstanding Showmanship in the 4-H Rabbit & Poultry Expo this summer. And although the spirits always say *everyone* is in love with Venus, after what Kyle Kellerman wrote in my memory book I'm feeling brave enough to finally ask what I really want to know.

I say, "Who does Kyle Kellerman like?"

The indicator spells out V-E-N-U-S.

Now, this really burns me up because I saw what Kyle Kellerman wrote in Venus's memory book and it was not that he liked *her* a lot. I've also started to get suspicious of that ouija board lately. I've even tested the indicator by not actually touching it, just making it *look* like I am, to see if maybe Venus pushes it, and it still moves even though the ouija regulations say the indicator won't work unless more than one person touches it.

That's when I decide to get even. I spell out Y-O-U C-H-E-A-T on the board.

"Who cheats?" Venus calls out to the spirits.

V-E-N-U-S, I write.

"How?" she huffs.

Y-O-U P-U-S-H I-T

I D-O N-O-T

L-I-A-R

L-O-S-E-R

C-H-E-A-T-E-R

D-U-M-B A-S-S

B-I-T-C-H

"Want to go play with my rabbits?" she asks.

"Fine," I say.

Later that summer, Venus and I have this sleepover at her house.

We watch *Happy Days* reruns and eat Cheetos and drink Orange Crush, then drag our pillows and blankets out on the patio after Charlene goes to bed and talk until Venus falls asleep first.

I'm alone in the dark after that, except for all these glittery stars spread out above me and some dogs barking in the distance, and I just lie there looking up at the sky and wondering if I will ever go out on a real date with Kyle Kellerman like the girls in poodle skirts on *Happy Days* whose boyfriends take them to Arnold's Place and Inspiration Point. Well, my stomach starts flopping all over the place just imagining it, but then I think about how Charlene used to cry in the back bedroom after Larry left and I want to know if Kyle Kellerman will ever make me sad like that because why bother if that's where you're going to end up? If I still believed in the ouija board I would ask the spirits about this, but in a funny sort of way it makes me feel better knowing it was only Venus pretending and that even though she always acts so sure about things, she doesn't know what's going to happen anymore than I do.

I guess you've just got to figure things out on your own, which is not that easy to do when Venus said she hated Kyle Kellerman but liked him all along, and Larry seemed so in love with Charlene but ran off with Tiffany instead. Even the things inside your own self are kind of a mystery if I can adore Venus one minute and ruin her hat the next, or hate my parents most of the time but feel so jealous of the fuss they make over Venus. But then I think about how Charlene smiles whenever this plumber named Frank stops by, and how Kyle Kellerman says he likes me even though Venus is prettier, and I decide maybe it's okay that what seems obvious isn't always right, like the night we drove home from spring break and my father said my mother had a lead foot, so my mother said my father had a big mouth, but when I reached over the front seat to grab a pillow it turned out they'd been holding hands the whole time.

Say Goodbye to Hollywood

"Sorry we're late," Irene called from the passenger's seat when the van rolled up to the curb where I stood waiting in the July heat. "Dipshit over here thought it would be a good idea to get the tires rotated." By *dipshit*, Irene meant her husband Pete, who shot me a withered look from behind the wheel. It was a look I knew well and one I met with as much sympathy as I could register without appearing to take sides, an expression I'd mastered in the year I'd been dating their son Kevin, who had jumped out the side door and was now loading up my suitcases. Their other son Brent was sacked out in the way back, and I smiled at him over the seat. "How's it going?" I asked, but Brent just stared at me as if the answer should be obvious. Brent hadn't planned to come along on this trip but he'd just broken into his former high school, fed the mice in the biology lab to the piranhas in the principal's office, and set off the fire alarm smoking a joint. His probation officer told Pete he shouldn't be left unsupervised, so he was along for the ride.

When Kevin climbed in beside me, he slammed the door, put his head in my lap, pulled me down and kissed me. "How's my girl?" he asked. I'd been a *girlfriend* twice when Kevin's smile had spun a ring of stars around my head in the Chemistry class I'd put off taking until senior year, but when I first heard him call me his *girl* – on the phone to a friend, asking if he could bring me to a party – I knew instantly that there was nothing more in the world I had ever wanted to be: not the ballerina I'd once aspired to, not the actresses I admired, not even the teacher I was studying to become and had always mentioned when anyone asked me what I wanted to be when I grew up.

But growing up was something Kevin had been accusing me of doing lately, and shopping for clothes in Marshall Field one afternoon, I discovered he was right. In the dressing room of the Juniors Department, the tee shirts and jeans I'd worn since I was a teenager no longer fit me, so I walked over to the Women's Department to look there instead. But while the pleated skirts and pantsuits I found had room for the hips and breasts that had finally asserted themselves on my too-thin frame, they didn't fit me in a different kind of way. They were clothes that announced just exactly who you were, something even I couldn't do since I wasn't even sure yet myself.

In my family, road trips were for games like "I spy" or counting broken headlights, my father telling stories about growing up in Arkansas, my mother teaching my sister and me to sing the Bob Dylan songs she'd learned in college. But an hour out of Grand Rapids, Irene was yelling at Pete who'd yelled at Irene for yelling at Brent to turn down his headset for chrissake did he want to go deaf, and although I had tried talking to Kevin about the fact that we were now moving to St. Louis together, where a minor league team had asked him to come play baseball after he'd lost his scholarship to the college where I'd just graduated, he'd mostly tried to ignore me.

Conversation wasn't one of Kevin's strengths, something everybody had seemed to notice about him right away except for me. But nobody else knew how the brush of his arm as we filed into class one day could say *I like you*, and the daisy he plucked for me when we filed out again *I know you like me too*. Nobody else knew how just the glance he gave me across the Wayside Tavern on our first date could tell me he knew things about me even I didn't know. I'd been sitting on a barstool while he ordered drinks with his teammates, watching their girlfriends blow smoke rings and toss back shots in their tiny little dresses and realizing I didn't stand a chance with Kevin since I normally spent my weekends studying to *Casey's Top 40* and filling out my little leather-bound planner in sweatpants, and that's when I saw it: that *look*, the one that told me I was more beautiful and mysterious and reckless than I'd ever imagined. And before I even knew it I was downing Cuervo and smoking cigarettes with his teammates' girlfriends and skipping classes for the first time in my life to sleep the mornings away in Kevin's arms, and months passed where I didn't care that it was hard to study for exams with half the baseball team in my living room or plan lessons for the first grade I was student teaching over Kevin's *Metallica*, because nothing mattered more to me than the fact that the beautiful, mysterious, reckless girl Kevin had seen across the Wayside that first night was *me*.

Then one night in April, he kept me awake watching a Tigers game before an interview I'd lined up at a nearby school. It was a job I really wanted, and I'd skipped the Wayside two weeks in a row to rehearse my demonstration, a fact that Kevin pointed to as evidence that I was "changing." By the night before the interview, all I needed was a good night of sleep, so I put a pillow over my head to drown out the sound, and when that didn't work, I tried earplugs. Finally, at one in the morning, I got up, put on a robe, and stood in the doorway of my bedroom, taking in the scene: the Rolling Rock bottles, the Domino's box, Kevin and his teammate Rob, awash in the light from the television.

"What?" Kevin asked.

"Tomorrow?" I reminded him.

Kevin gave me the glazed-over look that I'd noticed whenever I mentioned the interview, but after a minute he said, "Hey Robbie, my girl's gonna be a teacher."

Cecil Fielder struck out on the screen. "Aww, man," Rob said, then: "My mom's a teacher. That's cool."

I narrowed my eyes at Kevin and said, "It will be if I get the job."

And I did get the job. But when I drove over to tell Kevin the news at Pete and Irene's new house, where he'd been living in the spare room since flunking out, he wasn't home, which is the whole reason I ended up singing Billy Joel songs with Pete in the first place.

Pete had let me in that afternoon with a dusty guitar slung around his neck, and when we sat down in the living room, I said, "I didn't know you played."

"I found this in one of the boxes we never unpacked from the old house," he said. "I used to be in a band."

"No kidding," I said. Pete was a mechanic at a garage in Kalamazoo and I'd always imagined that that had been his only job.

"*Jet Stream*," Pete said. "That was our name. We played covers, mostly, but some of our own stuff too, even opened for Bob Seger once." He was smiling now. "We were pretty good." After a minute he said, "We were really good." He picked away at the guitar for a while, and I suddenly recognized the song he was playing.

"*Pick me up at the station, meet me at the train*," I sang.

Pete stopped. "You know 'Weekend Song'?"

"I love 'Weekend Song'," I said. "But Kevin only likes metal, so that's all I really listen to anymore."

Irene came up the stairs just then with a laundry basket, and Pete said, "Hey Irene, this kid knows 'Weekend Song'."

Irene gave Pete a look that said *deadbeat* and asked, "Aren't you supposed to be unpacking boxes?" But I'd always liked Pete. He was calm and laid back, always humming as he watered the hydrangeas or mowed the grass, and before my Corolla had given out in June, I used to find him underneath it, changing the oil or fixing a spark plug I hadn't even known was shot. He was thoughtful and patient and considerate, and when Irene went back downstairs he even remembered my interview and asked how it went, so I told him about the girl who wet her pants and the boy who threw up and the class rabbit that made a run for it in the middle of my demonstration on how to use the letter Q, but I could tell as we talked that Pete also heard what I wasn't saying: that in the midst of all that chaos, I felt like I was really good at something for the first time in my life.

When I finished talking, Pete walked into the kitchen to refill the coffee he was always drinking. "When do you start?" he asked. "August," I said, and when he returned, he'd poured a mug for me. Kevin always said coffee was for old folks and neither of us drank it, but when Pete handed me mine, he proposed a toast: "To August," he said, and we clinked mugs before I took the first sip and discovered I didn't hate it after all.

By the time we finished our coffee, Kevin still wasn't home, so Pete picked up his guitar and played a few notes of another song. "Why, Judy, Why," I said, so he played a few more of a different one. "Los Angelenos," I said, and then he tried to stump me with "The Great Suburban Showdown" but I guessed that one too. "You're good, kid," he told me, and we were having so much fun that I was disappointed when Kevin walked in, a deflated feeling that confused me because it was him I'd come to see all along.

Quitting the job was something I had intended to do ever since June, when Kevin had made the team and asked me to move to St.

Louis with him. It should have been easy enough to do: I'd already said goodbye to my roommates, turned in my keys to my landlady, packed my few belongings into the suitcases that were now piled up in the back of the van. But in spite of all this, I still hadn't told the school I was quitting yet, and the fact that I hadn't quit was something I hadn't told Kevin yet, either.

Now I was planning on calling the superintendent who'd hired me when we got to St. Louis in the morning. I had his number in my wallet, on the business card he'd handed me as he'd walked me to the parking lot after I'd signed the contract in May. When we'd passed the room full of kindergarteners who would be in my class next year, he paused at the door. "They'll be yours soon," he whispered, and he sounded so pleased about this that I couldn't help liking him.

But now that we were making the all-night push for St. Louis, I wanted answers to things I hadn't really thought through: Where would I find a job? I asked Kevin. What would we do about a car? When Kevin still didn't answer me, I gave up and watched the people who passed us in the fading light. One man picked his nose in his rearview mirror. A kid in a backseat held up a sign that said WAVE, so I did. Once, a woman looked like she was giving me the finger until I realized she was giving it to Brent, who was making obscene gestures out the window behind me with his tongue.

Brent had had a girlfriend for a while named Amber, and as we rode along in silence I couldn't help thinking how much more fun the trip would be if she was still around. Amber had been eight years older than Brent, twenty-seven to Brent's nineteen, a part-time hair dresser at a nearby salon. I'd first seen her playing with a slinky on the queen-sized mattress Brent had parked on the floor of Pete and Irene's den, which was doubling as a laundry room and had tripled as Brent's bedroom ever since he'd been fired from his job at Bonanza. Amber hadn't even asked who I was when she saw me on the stairs, just looked up and said, "Want to watch *CHIPs*?"

She had spiky black hair and a gravelly voice she never bothered to lower, which is why we always knew when Brent had skipped his latest interview or blown the money Irene had given him for the dentist on a lap dance at *Deja Vu*.

Maybe it was because she was older, but for some reason Irene had seemed happier with Amber around too. Irene had always been friendly to me in a distant kind of way, but with Amber in the picture, she'd started acting like the three of us were allies in what she called her "private war with men," which was really her "private war with Pete," and which wasn't as private as she seemed to think it was. Once, she'd given Amber and me little books filled with expressions like "A woman must work twice as hard as a man to be thought half as good – fortunately, this is not difficult" and "If you understand that most men are like children, you understand everything." She also loved to give advice about relationships in general, like the time she told us there was no point in breaking up with Kevin or Brent since one man was just as bad as another, though occasionally her advice was more specific, like the morning she told Amber she'd needed an ironing board from the den the night before, "but I knew you were down there with Brent," she said, "and I was afraid I might, you know, interrupt."

"No chance," Amber said. "Not when he's been drinking rum."

"Like father, like son," Irene told her. "Don't let him even think about scotch."

Now Irene was telling me not to even think about Coke at a truck-stop outside Gary, Indiana, where we'd pulled over to fill up, re-minding me that they'd had to stop three times for me to use the bathroom on the last roadtrip we'd taken to visit her mother in Peoria, so I put down the Big Gulp cup I'd been about to fill and hunted for something else to drink. I was thirsty, but it was caffeine

I really needed if I planned to stay awake, so even though the pot in the back of the store had a burned smell to it I poured myself a small coffee instead.

When I climbed back in the van, Brent wrinkled his nose at the steam from my cup. "What *is* that?" he asked.

"Coffee," I said.

"See?" Kevin snapped his fingers at Brent, as if this was proof of what he'd been saying about me all along, but the truth is that I wasn't really changing. It was more that being beautiful and mysterious and reckless had turned out to be a lot more work than I'd realized, and coffee helped lift the fog that late nights and tequila always left on my brain, something I'd discovered on the Saturday afternoons I'd been spending with Pete lately, afternoons when I showed up at the house well before I needed to meet Kevin, and Pete would get out his guitar and see how well I knew *Turnstiles* or *Street Life Serenade*. Then he'd tell me that "Scenes from an Italian Restaurant" is structured like an opera or that "The Entertainer" refers to "Piano Man," and Irene would tell Pete to get back to work, and I'd tell myself not to think about why I preferred hanging out with my boyfriend's father to hanging out with my boyfriend himself.

Three hundred miles from the Missouri border Brent lit up a cigarette, leaned forward, and blew smoke at the back of Irene's head.

"Not in the car, Brent," she said.

Brent took another drag. "When do we get to Mississippi?" he asked.

Brent was stupid, but for a while I'd thought at least Amber had been smart enough to break up with him after he'd slept with his new boss at Bennigan's. Then a few months later I happened to be driving down Amber's street and pulled over to say hello. Her hair was wet when she opened the door, and behind her I saw Brent wearing only a towel. Amber slammed the door on me and when she opened it again, Brent was pulling on a pair of pants and letting himself out the back door. "I have no idea what he's doing here," she told me.

I had no idea what he was doing there either, but then again I was starting to wonder what I was doing here, careening toward St. Louis with no job lined up and no car to drive when Pete and Irene left the next day. We didn't even have an apartment yet, something Kevin had said he'd look into before we left and then didn't, which meant we had no place to stay when we got there, and this had led to the first exchange we'd had in four hours on the road, but the truth is that it wasn't much different from any of the conversations we'd been having lately, which always ended up sounding like the one we were having now:

"I'll take care of it."

"I've heard that before."

"Will you just relax?"

"Fine," I said. "Great. I'll just relax."

"Why do you have to be like that?" Kevin asked.

"Like what?" I snapped. "Worried about *little things*, like a roof over our heads?"

"Yeah," Kevin said. "Like *that*."

"If you had half a brain," Irene jumped in now, "you'd be worried too."

"Ma," Kevin said.

"Don't *Ma* me," Irene said. "We can't keep bailing you out."

"Irene, they can handle it," Pete said.

"Oh, great," Irene sneered. "The oracle speaks."

"Just stay out of it," Pete said.

"Stay out of it?" Irene shrieked. "If I'd stayed out of it every time you told me to, nobody would have raised these kids." Irene was crying now. "Don't you even care what happens to him?" she asked.

"He's your *son*."

"I'm your son," Brent said. "How come I have to sleep on the floor?"

"You don't sleep on the floor," Pete said.

"You sleep on the floor," Irene said, "because your father wanted a garage instead of a third bedroom."

"Irene, that is not fair," Pete shouted.

"It is too fair," Irene cried. "It's the truth. You couldn't wait to get these kids out of the house, could you? Could you? Answer me," she sobbed, but instead of answering her, Pete slammed on the breaks, pulled over, and got out. We were somewhere near Indianapolis and stars spread over the cornfields as Pete took a pack of Marlboros out of his shirt pocket, fumbled with his lighter, and started walking along the highway until even his silhouette disappeared in the lights from the oncoming traffic.

Irene had a habit of making everyone else's problems her own, and it took a few minutes of listening to her sniffle in the dark to remember that the argument had actually been between Kevin and me, and I realized for the first time just how tired all of this was making me. All this time I kept hoping that the girl Kevin had seen across the Wayside that first night was the *real* me, the one underneath the *everyday* me, like a girl in a movie who turns out to be someone completely different when she takes her glasses off, but the truth is that I wasn't really beautiful or mysterious or reckless at all, and the only thing Kevin had really seen that night was the kind of girl we both wanted me to be. But acting like that girl wasn't just wearing me out – it wasn't even making Kevin love me the way I'd wanted him to anyway. Once, I'd even bought a little dress like the ones his teammates' girlfriends always wore, but when I'd worn it to his aunt's wedding in Detroit he spent the whole night throwing up the free shots from the open bar, and in the end only Pete asked me to dance with him, the person I never acted like anyone around but myself.

Back on the highway, the van was quiet except for the *Greatest Hits* cassette Pete had popped into the stereo. When he'd finally returned I'd switched seats with Irene, who'd started snoring almost immediately, followed by Kevin and then Brent, until their breathing leveled off, leaving only Pete and me awake in the dark.

"So," Pete said after a while. "It must have been hard to walk away from that job." When I didn't answer him, he said, "I should stay out of it, too. It just seems like you and Kevin aren't doing so well."

"We aren't," I admitted, "but the thing is," I started to say. Then I stopped. I'd wanted to give Pete a whole list of reasons why things weren't as bad as they seemed, but when I thought about it I could only come up with one, so I told Pete about the stars I still saw whenever Kevin smiled at me.

"I remember that feeling," Pete said. But he said this as if he were recalling fuzzy dice or leisure suits, some fad that had come and gone without him even noticing.

"You do?" I asked.

"Sure," Pete said. He thrust his chin back to where Irene was sprawled on the seat behind us. "She used to come watch me play. She'd stand right in the front row. It was all I could do to concentrate on the song I was singing."

This was hard to imagine, but I tried, and then something struck me. "Hey," I said, "Whatever happened to your band?"

"Oh, well, a lot of things," he said. "Mostly it was that I met Irene about the time the guys wanted to try and really make it, and I had to choose." Then he got quiet and stayed quiet for a long time, and although his hands were on the wheel and his foot was on the gas, I got the feeling that the rest of him was somewhere else, and this kept me quiet too.

When he finally spoke, he told me what it felt like to bring a room full of people to their feet, people who smiled and clapped and danced because of something he was doing up on the stage. He told me about the regulars who followed the band from bar to bar, who knew all the lyrics to the songs he'd written and used to sing along, and how great it all was, but that sometimes you make bad decisions when you're young because you don't really know what you're doing, and if someone could just tell you that you were making a mistake, if someone could just *tell* you, he said, it would save a whole lot of trouble for everyone, especially the kids you end up having who suffer for your mistakes and wind up in trouble no matter how hard you try and help them because you were too stupid to realize it was all going to turn out this way in the end.

When he was finished, I said, "So you're saying you'd like the chance to go back and make a different choice?"

"No," he said. He took his eyes off the road then and looked right at me. "What I'm saying is that you never get that chance."

Pete looked at me so long and hard that a truck driver blew the horn at him for drifting into the left lane, and when he swerved to get out of the way, Irene blinked and Kevin yawned and Brent stretched and sat up for a second. Then Pete turned up the music and began singing along to "Allentown," and because I knew our conversation was over, and because by now it was habit, I sang along with him. After a while, Kevin and Brent and Irene settled back down to sleep, but by then Pete and I were rolling as the little towns off the highway whizzed past us in the darkness: We had to be big shots. We tried for an uptown girl. We said goodbye to Hollywood. We left a tender moment alone. It was after three by the time I felt myself drifting off to the sound of tires on the uneven pavement and closed my eyes. When I opened them again, it was still dark outside, but I could tell by the way the stars were fading that it was almost morning.

Junior Lifesaving

The morning before Adam slips beneath the glassy surface of Lake Michigan, you find a letter from the woman you know he is in love with hidden in a closet of the house you are sharing for the summer. You are putting away a pile of his clothes that you have spot-treated and ironed, as if getting out all the stains and wrinkles will somehow fix things between you, when you see the sheets of stationery tucked behind a pile of socks, along with a carton of the Camels you didn't know he was still smoking. You are twenty-seven years old on a day you will replay over and over in your mind in the years to come, wondering, always, if you are to blame for losing him.

You met the woman once, his friend from college who tottered up on a pair of stilettos as you waited with Adam outside the Chicago Institute of Art. She was petite, blonde as a Barbie, thirty minutes late. Jessica. She draped herself around him – an embrace, or some version of it, that lasted the full six hours you were there – and went on about the number of marriage proposals she had turned down and the fact that people were always asking her if she was anorexic.

"Really?" Adam asked.

"Totally," she said.

You wandered among the galleries that day until Jessica confessed her ignorance about Seurat, and as Adam explained his work to her, you studied the three of you in the reflection of a tall glass case. Jessica, slender, fragile, diminutive, blinking her pale blue eyes. You, also slender, but strong instead of fragile, with limbs that seemed, next to hers, ungainly in their length, your curly red hair dingy and wild beside her smooth platinum light. Adam, shorter than you but taller than Jessica, coke-bottle glasses, black curls, his doughy arms and legs sticking out of his tee shirt and shorts.

Until that day, you had believed that he loved your discussions about postcolonialism and Pinochet and the collapse of the South African rand, conversations that began in the cafeteria when you met in law school two years before and led to the afternoon when you had argued about whether the first amendment should protect hate speech. You had been talking for a while before you noticed the way he was looking at you.

"What?" you asked.

"You're just so smart," he said before he looked away.

You had turned this over in your mind for weeks afterward, thought about the way he'd said it, softly, kindly, so different from the way your last boyfriend had spat the same words at you as you'd been breaking up. And so one night when he took off his glasses and leaned in to kiss you after you'd studied for an exam together, you let him, because he never seemed to mind your intelligence and competence, things you'd spent most of your life trying to conceal because you knew they were considered unattractive in women. In return, you didn't care that he had never played sports and had no idea how to change the oil in your car, or that once, when you sent him to get a wrench out of your hall closet, he came back with a pair of pliers. This became your unspoken pact, the deal you had struck. He forgave you your strengths, you forgave him his weaknesses.

And yet, even before you met her, you knew. Sometimes it was the way he said her name: *Jessica* is a dancer. *Jessica* is working on an advertising campaign for Colgate. *Jessica* is moving to Manhattan. And sometimes it was the way he didn't, like the time in the Japanese restaurant when he insisted you liked Miso soup and you said you'd never tried it.

He said, "I must be thinking of someone else."

You said, "Yes, you must be."

But at other times, unaccountably, almost meanly, he would make fun of her. *She's not exactly graceful*, he'd snort after seeing one of her recitals, or *What a mindless career, advertising*, and you would comfort yourself with the fact that he seemed not to take her seriously. But that day in the museum, watching him elaborate on Seurat's post-impressionist school of painting, on the illusion of a woman's face *here* or the corresponding technique on the frame *there*, you realized that it was this that should have worried you most of all.

By the time you were ten you had passed all of the swimming lessons offered at the local pool in the small Michigan town where you grew up, so your mother enrolled you in a class called Junior Lifesaving. It sounded boring until you showed up for the first class and fell in love with Tim the Lifeguard, who taught you how to inflate a wet pair of jeans by tying knots in the ankles and blowing into the waist to make your own flotation device.

You expected the class to be about saving other people but Tim the Lifeguard spent the first part of the summer teaching you basic water survival skills like treading water, floating on your back, and bobbing up and down. He said that you had to know how to protect yourself first before you could save anyone else. This was, he insisted, the number one rule of lifesaving.

～

The stationery is as delicate as she is and you know it is hers before looking at the signature because even cards from his ninety-year-old grandmother are tossed in the trash the minute he reads them. You hold it in your hands. Where were you when it came in the mail? Where did he sit when he read it? You try to picture the look on his face as he buried it behind the pile of socks. Guilty. The cigarettes he knows you hate confirm it.

You think: What kind of person reads someone else's mail?

Then you do it anyway.

You had lagged behind the two of them that day in the museum, sometimes disappearing in the maze of galleries so you wouldn't have to watch them, other times hoping he might notice your absence and come find you. One time, he did. You were standing in a room full of Goyas when he laced his fingers between yours to lead you back to where Jessica was waiting, but he dropped your hand the moment she was in sight. You wanted to say something then, to shout or scream that what she was doing – what he was allowing her to do – was not fair, not appropriate, not right. But instead, for days afterward, you cried in the car, in the shower, in the ladies' room, because you *couldn't*, because you had begun to understand that her total lack of substance and strength was her greatest asset. Defending yourself would have been pointless, or worse than pointless. There was nothing you could have said to Adam about this that would not have instantly served to make her even more appealing to him.

So now you let him win at Euchre. You pretend to know nothing about Mussolini so he can explain Italian fascism to you. When he slices his golf ball, you don't show him how to fix it. When he takes a wrong turn while you're camping on Lake Superior, you let him get good and lost and find his own way back, even though you knew the moment he veered left that he was supposed to veer right, even though it costs you an hour. And when you go crawfishing with strings and bits of raw bacon off a nearby pier, you secretly shake off most of what you catch so that he can drop more of the slimy creatures than you do into the bucket wedged between you on the dock.

"Lost another one," you say.

"Again?" he asks, but with a smile.

It works.

So the ticket you paid after you watched him park your car next to a fire hydrant, the concert you missed because he insisted it started at eight when you knew it started at seven, the sleep you lost when the hotel gave away your room because he miscalculated the distance to Detroit, a drive you'd made a million times growing up, and so you knew the whole six hours that there would be no room waiting for you when you arrived – these have seemed like small sacrifices to make compared with the pain of losing him.

But as you tuck the letter back behind the pile of socks, the kind of letter you wrote in the third grade to your cousin Jimmy – *Hi Adam. How are you? I'm fine. What have you been up to? I went to see a movie yesterday* – you realize that you still have a long way to go. In the vapid lines, you read your own failure at being the kind of girl he could really love, and you swear you will make yourself even more inane, more inept, more agreeable, if only he won't leave you.

This is what you are thinking when he drives you to the beach that evening, where you wash his hair for him like always, where he only ever goes in up to his waist, no further, because he does not know how to swim.

This is what you are thinking as he turns his back on the shore and begins to wade out to a deserted sailboat anchored a hundred yards away.

This is what you are thinking as you follow him instead of saying *stop* or *no* or *wait* or reminding him that he can't swim, as the smooth surface of the water rises over his waist, then his chest, then his neck, and he just keeps on going.

When you finally reached the unit on rescuing others, Tim the Lifeguard chose you to spend the hour splashing around in the center of the pool pretending you needed to be saved. The other students threw you ropes and life preservers and tried to drag you out of the water using poles with crooks on the end, and each time one of them succeeded, you had to swim back out and pretend you were drowning all over again.

But Randall Ridley, who was also ten and had terrible aim, gave up trying to save you by throwing things and dove in after you without a lifejacket.

Tim the Lifeguard blew his whistle.

"Stop," he said to Randall Ridley, who swam back to the side of the pool.

"What is the number one rule of lifesaving?" Tim the Lifeguard asked.

"Always protect yourself first," you all said in unison.

He told you, "Only the most experienced lifeguards can get that close to a drowning man and not lose their own lives in the process. A drowning man," he said, "will take you down with him."

Sixty yards offshore the water eases over your heads and Adam begins a palsied sort of paddle. His hands, gray with cold, break the surface in uneven strokes. At first you don't understand why his chin is held so high, but then you realize for the first time, with nothing to cling to but the chill around you, that he does not know how to hold his breath underwater.

He begins to pant. You are closer to the sailboat than to shore when you hear him sputtering as you swim ahead of him a few feet. If only you can make it to the boat, you think, he can rest. And you do make it to the boat. But there is nothing to hold on to once you get there, no ladder, no lines, no windows, no bars. You press your palms against the smooth fiberglass bottom. It arcs over where you float, and instead of stabilizing you, it glides away, your hands sinking into the darkness below.

Adam wheezes beside you. Against the nearness of the boat, it is as if the volume on his throat has been turned up, the nuance of panic in each breath suddenly distinct.

"Reach for the deck," you say.

You both reach for the deck, but miss it. You try again, kicking your legs and cupping your hands for resistance. You can hear Adam gurgling beneath you as you touch the edge of the boat but slide back into the water again.

You take a deep breath, cup your hands and kick again, and with one of the arms that had seemed so ungainly next to Jessica's, you reach the edge and grasp it. You dangle there, shaking too much to pull yourself up, so you hook the back of your heel over the edge, using your leg to lift you until you fall onto the deck.

But when you scramble up and look over the edge, Adam is gone.

Suddenly it is as if the world around you has frozen: the seagulls in midair, the speedboats mid-zoom, the cars on the gravel along the beach midway to their destinations. No dogs bark. No children yell. Everything stops moving and making noise.

How long do you stand there in the silence? Ten seconds? Fifteen? How long before a face breaks the surface below you, a face you don't recognize because it is so disfigured with fear? When you replay this moment in your head, you will pause here. It is like looking at someone you do not know, as if Adam disappeared into the water and a stranger emerged from it, a stranger whose voice is high and thin and desperate.

"Help me!"

But when you look around the deck, there is nothing to throw to him, no rope, no pole, no life preserver. So with one hand you grip a guardrail and pitch forward with your head and chest and waist and hips until you throw your body off the boat to offer him your other hand.

⤧

Adam does not look at you the next morning at breakfast, nor the next evening at dinner, nor again as he spends his days at a separate job and his nights on a separate side of the bed, always saying *yes* and *fine* to your polite questions about what he wants for dinner or how his day went during the two weeks that pass before he packs up his things and moves out.

What if you had waited? What if you had given him more time to follow your lead? What if he really could have saved himself? What if. All you know for sure as you stand in the driveway and watch his red taillights vanish in the distance is that what you feared the day he almost drowned has come true anyway. You will never see him again.

That night, you choke down the leftovers of the spaghetti you made for him the night before. You wash and dry your one plate and one cup and one fork and one spoon. You change into your nightgown. And after you've cried yourself to sleep, you realize that your body is drifting in the currents at the bottom of the bay where shards of green sunlight filter around the sailboat that floats above you. Soggy playing cards are strewn across the lake floor. Seagulls that can fly underwater duck in and out between your limbs. And you think you must be swimming until Tim the Lifeguard glides past to say you broke the number one rule of lifesaving.

Endless Caverns

It was a trip Sarah had been avoiding, and now it was raining, thick cords of water snaking down her windshield as she headed north to the little town where Grace had grown up, and where she had moved with the boys after the accident. Sarah had been so dreading the trip that she had even considered making a last-minute excuse, but the look Dan gave her over breakfast when she mentioned this had her packing her overnight bag, which now sat in the back seat of the car as she neared the Winchester exit. The drive up from Charlottesville had been filled with reminders of happier times: the turnoff for Skyline Drive where they'd all hiked fifteen miles together, the billboard for the Waffle House where Eli had taught them how to eat hash browns *smothered*, *covered* and *chunked*, the sign for the caverns they'd visited the last time Sarah and Dan had seen Eli alive, its tall white letters standing out against the green mountainside like the letters that spelled out HOLLYWOOD.

At the funeral three months before, questions had swirled about the accident – a head-on collision with a tractor-trailer – but no one seemed to know why Eli had crossed the yellow line. Had he been avoiding a pot hole? A rabbit? A dog on the side of the road? Had he been fiddling with the GPS? The radio? His cell phone? Eli had died instantly, so no one could ask, though the afternoon Grace had called to deliver the terrible news she had described to Sarah the dream she'd had after identifying his body at the hospital.

In it, she had been walking behind Eli, asking why he'd swerved, but he had only mumbled without turning around so she could not hear his answer.

At the Winchester exit, Sarah followed the directions Grace had given her to the new house, but when it stayed quiet even after she'd pressed the doorbell, Sarah checked them again. She was retracing her steps when Grace appeared at the door in jeans and a tee shirt, bonier even than she'd been months earlier when Sarah had searched for her at Eli's visiting hours and realized with a shock that she was the woman in the navy blue dress standing unnaturally still in the corner while people spoke in hushed voices and dabbed at the corners of their eyes.

"Come in," Grace said simply, and closed the door behind Sarah. "The boys will be happy to see you."

Sarah had first met Eli and Grace years before, when the medical resident she was dating had taken her to their house for a barbeque. Jack was a colleague of Eli's at the hospital in Charlottesville, and while they waited for Eli to return from the kitchen with their drinks, it occurred to Sarah that she had never felt so immediately welcome anywhere as she did at their house, a place that was filled with motion and laughter and life: Eli and Grace, their three little boys on the swing set, two Danish spaniels tugging on a stick, and a German exchange student kicking a soccer ball around the yard. And Grace was five months pregnant with their fourth child. She was tall and willowy with thick brown curls and a long, graceful neck, setting places at the picnic table where they'd eaten, the four of them, laughing when the soccer ball got wedged in the branches of the maple, marveling when the spaniels stole a bratwurst right off the flaming grill, chatting until the sun went down and the mosquitos came out.

But the medical resident had vanished after that night, and when Sarah had spotted him having dinner with one of his nurses at a noodle house in Charlottesville, she assumed she'd never see Eli or Grace again. So she was surprised when her phone rang later that week and it was Eli on the other end. "I'm sorry about Jack," he'd said simply. "Come to dinner." And so Sarah had walked the six blocks to their house, and while Grace floated around the back yard, tending to the boys, Eli stood at the grill, a spatula in one hand and a beer in the other, tall, bearded, smiling. Watching them together, Sarah thought, it was as if they communicated telepathically: without notice, Grace had a plate ready for each steak Eli pulled off the grill, and without looking, Eli seemed to know a plate would be there, and in this way they carried on their conversation with Sarah and the exchange student uninterrupted, except when the children played too loudly or one of the dogs strayed into a neighbor's yard.

A week later, they had invited Sarah out for Mexican where the boys had hijacked the waitresses' sweepers and had run up and down the aisles with them, and a week after that they'd gone to the movies together – Grace, Eli, Sarah, and the German exchange student – in the brand new minivan that Sarah would ride in a million times and later see smashed to pieces in the newspaper story about Eli's death. As Eli had struggled to wedge the van into the only empty spot on the parking lot of the theater, a tiny space between a lamppost and a badly parked Hummer, he had grinned and said, "It's like trying to have sex with a pregnant woman," and Grace – almost six months along by then – had howled as loudly as the rest of them.

But no matter where Grace and Eli took her, Sarah remained fascinated by their ability to predict one another's next move. At the tangle of trails in Pocahontas State Park, when Eli disappeared with Christopher, Grace guessed exactly which paths he'd taken and tracked him down. At the Dairy Queen, when Grace had taken Alex to the bathroom, Eli ordered Grace a double dip of Mint Chocolate Chip and Chocolate Peanut Butter which turned out to be exactly what Grace had wanted. And at their house, where Sarah became a regular fixture, Grace could predict the exact moment Eli would pull into the driveway no matter what shift he was working, just as Eli seemed to know exactly what Grace needed from the store without ever having been told. Once, when Grace had been fixing dinner, she realized she'd forgotten to buy shallots for the stir fry, but when Eli walked through the door, he'd reached into a small paper sack and produced a little bag of them, which Grace had chopped without comment, and – as if this kind of mind-reading was not the miracle it seemed to Sarah – tossed them into the pan, and called the boys to supper.

Now they stood in the kitchen of the new house, where Grace began molding hamburger into patties as she told Sarah about the kids' new school and Caleb's great soccer coach and how Winchester hadn't changed a bit since she'd been away, and Grace was so talkative as Sarah chopped vegetables for the salad that she kept forgetting that Eli wasn't just at work, wasn't going to walk through the door as he had always done after those late afternoons back in Charlottesville, interrupting Grace and Sarah's chatter with a story about his day that had them in stitches, while the children jumped and shouted and shimmied up his massive frame until he'd kissed each one hello.

Sarah had expected the boys to be altered in some visible way when she had arrived that afternoon, but when Grace had led her downstairs to see them, they had shouted hello from little battery-operated four wheelers as they careened around the unfinished basement, uproarious as ever, and as Sarah had peered into each of their little faces, she had wondered just how much they understood.

Then Grace had led Sarah through the house, pointing out the family room, the living room, and the back porch, after which they'd headed upstairs, where Sarah had dropped her bag in the guest room. As they walked down the hall, Grace had continued the tour. "This is Liam's room," she said. "Chistopher's here, Alex is there." Another room: "That's Caleb's." Then she had pointed to a door at the end of the hall. "And mine." *Mine.* Sarah had winced at the word.

This was not the house Grace had planned on. Why, just that spring Sarah and Dan had driven to the countryside beyond Charlottesville with Eli and Grace to see the property where they were planning to build. It had been a beautiful morning in May as they followed Eli and Grace through the tall grass into the walnut grove where they'd pointed out the little orange flags that marked the parameters of their property and discussed the house they were designing together. Then Eli had grabbed Dan and they'd run over to the old barn on the back of the acreage, where, like children, they had pushed a giant tractor tire up a hill, just to let it roll down again, just to watch it tumble and bounce and break through a fence Eli said he was planning to take down anyway.

With the boys sealed off in the basement now, there was a terrible stillness in the house that seemed to grow more silent even as Grace went on about how nice it was to be back in Winchester and the horseback riding lessons she'd signed up for and the live-in nanny she'd hired whom the boys adored, and though Sarah had begun to feel as if they should be talking about the obvious matter at hand, she let Grace take the lead, though she struggled to come up with responses more complex than *wow* and *no kidding* or *that's great.* And it was the same when dinner was ready: the boys sat around the table while Grace asked Christopher about his math test and

Alex about his Game Boy and Caleb and Liam about their Sunday School teacher, and the entire meal passed without a single reference to Eli, though he seemed more present somehow in his absence than he'd ever been when he'd sat at the head of the table, asking Grace to pass the ketchup or wiping his beard with his napkin.

After dinner, Grace put the boys down for the night, and when the nanny – a pleasant-faced twenty-year-old from a nearby college – returned from her day of classes, Grace asked if Sarah wanted to take a walk. So they donned sweaters and scarves and headed out into the chilly November night to walk along the railroad tracks under the stars that had emerged after the rain had passed, and Grace talked about putting pennies on the track as a child just to watch the trains flatten them, and walking here with the first boy she'd ever kissed in eighth grade, and the geometry teacher she'd had a terrible crush on, who still taught at the same high school, and how she sometimes ran into him at Costco now that she was back home again.

When they reached town, they found a dimly lit bar and took a seat far from the other customers, and it was there that Grace, who had been talking for almost an hour without stopping, lapsed into silence.

"So how are you holding up?" Sarah asked. It was what she'd been wanting to know since her arrival, but something Grace, with all her chattiness, seemed to be trying to prevent her from asking, and now Grace looked out the window for so long that Sarah wasn't sure she'd even heard her.

"I'm still here," Grace finally said, but she kept her eyes on the street. "I guess that's something."

"Do they know what happened yet?" Sarah asked, meaning the accident itself, the reason Eli swerved. But even as she said it, she wasn't sure who *they* were. The police? The road commission? The auto body shop that had hauled the minivan away? Still, *they* was a less direct word than *you*, so Sarah used it.

When Grace didn't answer for real, Sarah said, "I still can't believe it. I know accidents happen, but I just keep thinking it could have been avoided. It was such a freak thing, you know?" Something passed across Grace's face that Sarah couldn't read, and it was then that she felt herself starting to ramble, about the article she'd read on the spike in car accidents now that everyone used cell phones, and how distracted people were compared with ten years ago, and how multitasking had become this huge problem, when Grace reached across the table for her hand and said, "Sarah."

"I mean, it just really made me think . . ."

"*Sarah*," Grace said, and Sarah felt something sink inside her.

"What?" Sarah asked, her throat gone suddenly dry.

Grace looked at her evenly, but spoke gently. "It wasn't an accident."

Sarah blinked. "What do you mean?"

"It wasn't an accident." And Grace went on to explain that Eli had not had his cell phone with him. That the road commission had found no potholes in the highway. That the driver of the tractor-trailer, who had jumped from the wreck and survived, but whose rig had not, bursting into flames, the gas tank exploding, had seen no rabbit or deer or squirrel in the road. What he'd seen instead was Eli, wrenching the steering wheel deliberately into his path. And there was more: Eli's history of depression, the medications he'd been taking for years, the night, two years ago, when he'd tried to jump off the Interstate 64 bridge.

When Grace finished, Sarah could not form any words. Protesting would have been pointless, given Grace's firmness. Saying "I'm sorry" did not go nearly far enough. And suggesting that it *still* could have been an accident – something Sarah clung to, unable to believe that Eli could have left Grace and the boys in such a terrible lurch, unwilling yet to convict him of this if there was even the slightest chance he might be innocent – seemed cruel in and of itself, given how much the possibility, however remote, might torture Grace. But the Eli Sarah had known had been so happy, so sane, so *normal*, that awful word her parents sometimes used as to differentiate between themselves and people who ate sushi or got divorced. But here, it applied: Eli had always seemed so *normal*.

"But you know what really gets me," Grace was saying now, "is that people seem to think I should have *known*." And Sarah felt a pang of guilt, because she realized that as Grace had been talking, she had been thinking the same thing. "But if I had, don't you think I'd have tried to stop him?" And Sarah, suddenly shivering, could only nod and pull her sweater tighter around her shoulders as the news settled over her. Of course Grace would have tried to stop him. Of course she didn't know.

Grace leaned forward now, all her quiet firmness dissolved. "Do you know what Eli did that morning?" Her eyes filled as she spoke. "He ate Cheerios for breakfast. He took a shower and dressed for work. He dropped the kids off at school. I'm not even sure *he* knew what he was going to do right up until the moment he did it. How on earth was I supposed to?"

As she drove back to Charlottesville the next morning, Sarah thought about the last time she'd seen Eli alive. They'd all eaten lunch together at a new open-air Italian place, where Eli had debated the Yankees vs. the Red Sox with Dan, raved about the seafood linguine, managed one of Caleb's meltdowns with his usual patience and humor. It was a marvelous afternoon in late August, clear and cool, and Sarah would not know until after Eli's accident just how vividly she'd been able to picture the days they would all spend together in the future, the years stretching lazily before them, just waiting to be filled with picnics and hikes and enormous meals like the one they'd only just finished.

Then, after settling the bill, they had caravaned up Highway 81 behind Eli and Grace and the boys to Endless Caverns. Sarah still remembered the chilly sensation of descending into the earth, and the story the guide told them about the caverns sitting undiscovered beneath the lush Virginia farmland for centuries until some children chasing a rabbit saw the creature disappear into a windy hole. She remembered too that when Eli had asked why they were called *endless*, the guide had explained that after years of expeditions, geologists still did not know where the caverns ended – no matter how far they explored, the tunnels just kept going. And Sarah remembered how that tour had made her think differently about the ground that had always been beneath her feet. It wasn't all concrete or topsoil, green grass or wildflowers. There was a whole world under there, one that snaked and burrowed, widened and narrowed, darkly mysterious, unfathomably deep.

Personal Space

To get to Rome from Urbino by train, you have to take a bus to the station in Pesaro, which is where I meet him, Scottish brogue and boyish, boarding the 6:05 to Bologna, where I'll catch my second train. On the platform he tells me his name is Alan, asks where I'm from, teases me about my accent, not just American, but midwestern to boot, my vowels Michigan-long and nasal. When we've put our bags in the overhead bins, I pick a seat by the window and begin the first leg of a journey that will carry me to the Eternal City, to the man who waits for me there, to the Sistine Chapel where we're headed this afternoon. For months I've seen my favorite panel, *The Creation of Man*, drawn by graffiti artists on the sidewalks of Verona and Florence and San Marino, but today I'm finally going to see the original painted by Michelangelo.

My immediate plan is to gaze at the sun coming up over the Adriatic until the train veers inland, but Alan sits down next to me, rambling about rugby and American baseball and the former colleague from Glasgow he saw last night in Ravenna until I open up the window to let in some air.

"Thank you," he says.

"No problem," I say.

"*No problem*," he repeats, only in his brogue it comes out *new p-r-r-roblem*. "Why can't Americans ever just say 'You're welcome' or 'My pleasure'?"

"I'm not sure," I tell him. "I never thought about it before."

"Why mention the 'problem' bit," he asks, "like it might actually be one after all?" But since I can't answer this question either, and since the universal sign for *I don't want to talk anymore* is cracking open a book, I pull out the volume of Calvino's *Marcovaldo* I'm trying to finish without a translation dictionary and read for a while. But just when I'm starting to get somewhere, Alan reaches across me for a copy of *La Nazione* someone left on the floor, and when I automatically pull my leg away from the sudden threat of contact with his arm, he sighs.

"That's another thing," he says. "Why do you Americans need so much personal space?"

I don't know if what Alan says is true of all Americans, but I know what is true about me: in hallways and subways and crowds on the street, I keep a buffer around me at all times, two or three feet of space I obtain by reading the movements of people nearby and then speeding up or slowing down, stepping left and then right to avoid contact, maneuvers that are so second nature I never really thought about them until I moved to Italy and people kept cutting in front of me at the *fruttivendolo* or *farmacia* thinking I wasn't in line. I equate physical contact with intimacy, the kind that is reserved solely for lovers, like the one I'm on my way to meet this afternoon, which is why I'm always unnerved by friendly handshakes, avoid the casual grazing of shoulders on airplanes, refuse even the anonymous arm offered to steady me when I've stumbled.

Alan is still waiting for my answer, and I want to give him a simpler one, to tell him that space is a form of politeness back home, a way of not encroaching on other people, but politeness seems a hollow excuse when I have the distinct impression I've just been rude, and so instead of answering him, I smile and shrug, annoyed now, or embarrassed, I'm not sure which, and turn back to *Marcovaldo*, though the question hangs in the air of our compartment like smoke that never clears.

When the train finally pulls into Bologna I shove my book in my bag and nod goodbye to Alan, glad to be free of these questions I can't answer. But in my haste to escape him, the heel of my shoe catches on the top step of the train and my body pitches forward, the contents of my purse falling around me. Then I'm falling too, the stairs gone beneath me, the train upside down, until I crash onto the platform below, the beads from my necklace scattering like marbles.

But when I try to stand up, the station whirls into blackness. The next thing I see is a gray ceiling. I'm inside a van, moving somewhere, the blip-blip-blip of a siren blaring, a paramedic working over me. Behind him I see Alan, smiling as I blink.

In a hallway of the emergency room he stands beside my gurney talking with the admissions staff, filling out my paperwork, handing over the passport he fishes from my bag. He tracks down a pillow for my head, begs a blanket off an orderly, negotiates with the nurses for something that will stop me writhing in pain. He trades a bill from his wallet for the coins in someone's pocket, slips them into a vending machine, hunts for a straw to help me drink. Then he calls the man I'm meeting in Rome to tell him I'll be late, a man who bristles and rages and does not want to know how I am, only just exactly what Alan is doing with me, and when Alan puts the phone down, the look he gives me says he'd like to know just exactly what I'm doing with the man who just hung up on him. But he doesn't ask, and for this I am grateful: it would be just one more question I don't have an answer for.

Six hours later, there's a cast on my leg. Alan carries my bag while I work the crutches a doctor has given me, a doctor who has told me I'm young and strong and healthy and should feel better soon, and as we sit in the restaurant across from the station, eating steaming plates of pasta I've insisted on buying since it's the least I can do, Alan gives a jokey translation of the doctor's prognosis: "You're young and strong and ugly," he tells me. "You're going to be just fine."

I say, "You must have had somewhere else to be."

"Not really," he tells me, and when I ask where he was headed, he says, "Back to Glasgow."

"Why are you in Italy?" I ask, something that never came up in the scurry and shuffle of the emergency room, and when he doesn't say anything right away, I wonder if I've actually stumbled upon a question *he* can't answer.

"My wife doesn't want me at home," he finally says.

He looks up at me then, and I know not to ask anything more. Instead, I think of him, a complete stranger, sitting beside my gurney all day, handing me napkins from the cafeteria until the painkillers kicked in and I finally stopped crying, and I can't imagine who on earth wouldn't want a husband so kind. I also can't imagine that the man I'll sleep next to in Rome tonight will ever be as kind to me as Alan has been today, or why, when I know this, I'm still meeting him there anyway, which is why after Alan and I have walked back to the station, I hug him goodbye, and he lets it pass without a single joke, leaning into me silently until the whistle blows. After he climbs aboard the train that will carry him to Milan and his flight back to Glasgow, I sit down on a bench to wait for the next train to Rome, but when I look up again, Alan is waving to me out the window. The engine has started to roar.

"Thank you," I shout over the racket.

Through the glass he mouths, "No problem."

I watch his train until it disappears in the distance. My own train is due any minute, and when it pulls into the station, I hook my bag over my shoulder and half-wobble-half-hop to the nearest open doorway. Above me a conductor is taking tickets, but I don't know how I'm going to make it up those stairs.

"Posso aiutarla?" the conductor says when he sees me. *Can I help you?* And when he reaches down and offers me his hand, I take it.

The Club

Gladwin High School's cheerleading coach Glory Jo Baker says she'd recognize spirit a mile off, and Glory Jo Baker would know. She used to cheer for the Detroit Lions until she broke her collarbone doing a back hand spring, so everyday at practice I jump and shout and shake those pom-poms like crazy, even though I have to work twice as hard as the thinner girls whose toe touches and pikes are always so clean. Plus there are only six open spots on the squad this year since Kaylee Ritchart and Kristin Banks are back. They're both blonde and thin and tan year-round from lying in the beds at Malibu Sun & Nails, and sometimes Glory Jo will turn practice right over to them. She'll say, "Show them the Victory Vault while I get myself a Diet Coke." Then Kaylee and Kristin model it for us, and it's like they're not even trying but it all comes out perfect anyway.

Tryouts are only a month away, so I fit in extra practice at home whenever I can. I go over the rules in the Cheerleading Handbook and rehearse every new cheer ten times *at least*. Sometimes I line my stuffed animals up on the couch and practice making eye contact with the crowd so I'll get high marks on Natural Charisma, but my father always says the crowd better be off the couch by the time Peter Jennings comes on.

And I was really making progress until a few weeks ago when my grandmother Mayzee and her pomeranian Uncle Jasper moved in. Mayzee's so confused she can't remember anything anymore, so now we have to cut her fingernails and tuck her in to bed and walk Uncle Jasper three times a day. And every morning we have to put Mayzee's dentures in and give her a bath and dress her, which is a lot harder than it sounds since she doesn't recognize any of her clothes anymore. My mother will hold up the yellow polyester pantsuit Mayzee's been wearing for like a million years and Mayzee will just stand there looking steamed. She'll say, "I will *not* wear those old hand-me-downs."

Still, I just *have* to find time to get those cheers right, so I finally gave up the cello lessons Rosemary Fuller and I have been taking for years, even though I love the cello more than anything and was just getting the hang of my double stops. Rosemary has been my neighbor since age three when her family moved in across the street, and she was real disappointed when I told her I was quitting, but to tell you the truth, it's kind of a relief not to have to haul my cello case to school every day. I mean, at Gladwin High School, you might as well just drag around a big flashing *loser* sign. But for some reason this never seems to bother Rosemary one bit. She just sits there with that big honking case next to her like she's committing social suicide right there on the bus, but I guess when you have a retarded brother who takes off his bathing suit at the Gladwin Public Pool, nothing fazes you. Which is probably why Rosemary never breathed a word to anybody about the time my father and his drinking buddies stripped off their hunting suits and stood around the front yard doing turkey calls in their underwear.

Trying out for cheerleading also means I don't have time to study my Spanish verbs either, which is too bad since I really want to impress Wendell Biggs, who asked me to be his conversation partner last week. I said: "How are you?" and Wendell said: "I'm fine. And you?" And I said, "Oh, great." But since it's just Beginning Spanish, the only other thing we could really do was order Cokes from a fake waiter, which made it seem like we were supposed to be on some kind of date, and the only thing I could remember after that was the word for *airport*. I swear my brains just go to mush around that kid. Once, when I was working at Clayton's Diner last summer, Wendell told me I was a great waitress, and all I could think to say was, "Clayton gets our cold cuts from Detroit." But I guess Wendell didn't care because he was there for lunch again the next day. And the next. Once he was even outside on his moped when I got off work, so he gave me a ride home, and we stood in the driveway where Wendell told me about his high-powered telescope and I told Wendell about making first chair in cello last year, and Wendell told my father how nice our lawn looked, but my father just said, "God, I am not ready for this."

It is my dream to dance with Wendell at the first school mixer, which is coming right up. I just pray he will ask me. I imagine it every time a slow song comes on the radio: he'll put his hands around my waist and I'll put my hands around his neck, and we'll dance in this perfect sync where nobody steps on anybody's toes, and in my dream the song we dance to is so long that it never stops playing.

Now, for weeks I have been begging my mother to let me tan at Malibu Sun & Nails like Kaylee and Kristin do, but my mother just says she did not give up Ernest and Julio Gallo for nine months so her daughter could look like a handbag. Still, she does take me to see her hairdresser Nadine who dyes my hair blonde and straightens it all out for me, but when she spins me around in the chair so I can get a look at myself in the mirror, my head looks kind of shrunken without all those curls. Nadine says I'll get used to it after a few minutes, and I sort of do, once I stop expecting to see myself there.

But the next day at practice, my new hairdo is a big hit with

Glory Jo, who says I look exactly like Daryl Hannah, and Kaylee and Kristin even ask me to start hanging out in the girl's bathroom with them during lunch instead of eating in the cafeteria with Rosemary. Well, we just have a *ball* practicing cheers in front of the mirrors and painting each other's nails the same pink as Glory Jo's, but what I really wish I knew is how those two go all day without eating. I mean, throwing out my peanut butter and jelly almost kills me, and even when the hunger pains don't get me, I just about drown in a pool of my own guilt thinking of how tired my mother looks when she gets up early just to fix it for me. Lucky for me, Grandma Mayzee won't eat unless we make her, so every morning we shake those cereal boxes around and make a bunch of noise about how good they all are, and all that fuss takes the focus off the fact that I just sort of stir my cereal around anymore until it's time to get on the bus.

Now, I just hate riding the bus, all those wads of chewed up gum stuck everywhere and those windows covered in dirty handprints. But at least it gives me a chance to catch up with Rosemary since I don't really see her at school anymore. But one morning when I sit down across from her, she looks real upset. So I say, "What is it, Rosemary?" And Rosemary says, "I'm auditioning today and Nancy Biddle was supposed to be my page turner but she's sick." Now Rosemary and I used to make fun of Nancy Biddle, who has these giant glasses that make her eyes bug out and is so persnickety she's like a little old lady trapped in the body of a fifteen year-old, but ever since I've quit cello, Rosemary can't stop yapping about Nancy's left-hand technique. Sometimes I just want to shake her and say, "Geez, Rosemary, keep it *down*." I mean, it's one thing to still drag your cello around once you're in high school, but it's another to go around bragging about Nancy Biddle like that.

Then Rosemary gets this hopeful look on her face and says, "Could you stand in for her? It would only take a minute, and my mom can give you a ride home." And because Rosemary's voice wobbles so much, I say, "Sure, Rosemary. I'll be there." Well, she looks like she might cry, she's so grateful. She says, "You are a real friend, Jenny. I just knew I could count on you." Which only makes me feel worse about the fact that I sometimes pretend not to see her in the hallway, depending on who I'm walking with.

So when the end of the day comes, I'm packing up my book bag to head for Rosemary's audition, but the next thing I know I see Kaylee coming my way. And she lights right up when she sees me and says, "Hey Jen, want to ride over to the Wagon Wheel with me?" And just the way Kaylee calls me *Jen* is so natural and friendly that before I even know how it's happened, I'm flying down Mission Street in Kaylee's zippy little RX-7. And when we get to the Wagon Wheel, Rodney Stanger is waiting outside for us with Chad Harmon. Rodney is Gladwin's star quarterback whose varsity ring Kaylee wears wrapped up in yarn so it'll fit her tiny little hand, and Chad has these big shoulders and this jaw like Superman, and even though Rosemary says they're both as dumb as a box of rocks, it really knocks me out just to be standing in line with them.

Well, we all order sodas and grab a booth and sit around talking about *Who's the Boss?* And *Alf* and *America's Funniest Home Videos* until Kaylee tells Rodney she loves him, and Rodney says he loves her *more*, and Kaylee says she loves *him* more, and pretty soon the thrill wears off and I start feeling just awful about Rosemary. I can picture her in the band room with her cello. I can see the worry on her face as it dawns on her that I'm not coming. And suddenly my heart starts pounding and my throat gets dry and I suck down my Diet Coke so fast it gives me a headache. Then I realize I don't even know how I'm going to get home, so I excuse myself and go call my mom at work from a pay phone.

It takes *forever* for her to get there, and all I want to do is cry when she pulls up. I want to hunker down in the back of that big old Chrysler and wail. But instead she sends me in to pick up Mayzee from this wing of the Gladwin Hospital where we take her when no one's home. Everyone else at that place is just as confused as Mayzee is, and they sit around all day while this lady reads them *Nancy Drew* or *The Boxcar Children*, or leads them in singing Christmas carols, even though it's only September. It's called Adult Day Care, but whenever you ask Mayzee where she spent the day she says she was at *the club*. "The Club," my mother always laughs. "Like they're playing tennis and sipping martinis all day." But Mayzee's so happy whenever we drop her off that she lights up like Miss America and waves at everyone, even though Melva Jenks starts cursing the minute she walks in. But it's like Mayzee doesn't even hear her. You'd think it was the Kennedys sitting there from the way Mayzee acts, instead of a bunch of people who can't remember their own names watching *Jeopardy* and drooling into their milkshakes.

I swear Mayzee's gotten worse in just these last couple of weeks. It's so bad that she doesn't always recognize us anymore. She can't even remember Uncle Jasper half the time. Sometimes that little puff ball will come nosing on into the TV room while Mayzee's watching *The Price is Right* and she'll say, "What the hell is that?" And we'll say, "Mayzee, it's Uncle Jasper," but she just looks at us all like we're nuts.

Now, tryouts are only one week away when Señora Murphy hands back our first Spanish tests. As if getting a *D*+ isn't bad enough, it's even worse with Wendell sitting behind me, holding onto his own *A*, asking how I did. But when I tell him, he just says I'll do better next time and asks me to be his conversation partner anyway, so he asks me where one might buy a newspaper and I ask him where one might buy the best clams, and the whole time Wendell is looking at me in this way that makes me just float through the rest of my classes. But when I get on the bus at the end of the day I can feel

Rosemary boring a hole in the back of my head just like she does everyday anymore. And what for? She got first chair without me turning her pages anyway. Which makes me feel kind of sick if I think about it for too long.

But who needs Rosemary when Kaylee and Kristin have invited me to get ready for the school mixer with them on Friday? All week I have been thinking about how great it will be to walk into that gymnasium with them. But when my mother drops me off at Kaylee's in my best jeans and the pink sweatshirt I bought when we took our vacation to New Jersey, she and Kristin give each other these *uh-oh* looks and say why don't they lend me some clothes? And I say great, since I've lost so much weight that none of my clothes really fit me anymore, and the next thing I know I'm wearing Kristin's mini-skirt and this slinky black top and a pair of these strappy black heels that are a size too small. And a bunch of Kaylee's makeup, only on me all those colors and lines seem kind of clownish and loud. But Kaylee and Kristin go on about how it brings out my features, and I'm glad they think I look so much better, only the more they say it, the more it's like they're saying I wasn't okay before, and then I start to worry that I won't be able to figure out how to put it on even after I go out and buy it all, which of course I will since Glory Jo says you cannot stop trying to improve yourself or you will never get married.

Well, by the time we get to the mixer those high heels have already given me two blisters and the music hasn't even started yet. But then the DJ plays *La Bamba*, and Kaylee and Kristin and I start dancing to *Addicted to Love*, and by the time *Mony Mony* comes on I've just about got the knack of those shoes after all. Then the DJ slows things down with *Purple Rain*, and all of the sudden, out of the corner of my eye, I see Wendell walking toward me. And my stomach gets all fluttery because I just *know* he's going to ask me to dance.

But as he gets closer, this funny thing happens: it's like I start to see all these things about him I've never noticed before, like how skinny he is and the way he parts his hair down the middle and buttons his shirts all the way up. And suddenly I'm not even sure I think he's cute. I mean, that boy wouldn't know a football if it hit him in the head.

So I just keep talking to Kaylee like I don't even see him coming. But Kaylee says, "Hey, don't you know him?" And I say, "Who?" And Kaylee says, "That *smart* kid." Only she says it in this way that means I better think up something quick or I'm *out*. So I say, "He does my homework sometimes." Which is a lie, but Kaylee and Kristen get a big laugh out of that. They say, "Oh, will he do ours too?" And just like that, I'm back in.

But then I see Wendell's face as he veers past me. He looks like the air has been sucked out of him, and he's shrinking by the second. Then my eyes start to sting because I don't know why I'm acting this way. I've never been so mean in my whole life, and before I can even think how to fix this, Chad Harmon walks up and asks me to dance. But the whole time we're out there, Chad keeps saying how pretty I look, which for some reason really gets on my nerves. And a few days later, after I finally make the cheerleading squad and Glory Jo issues me my official Gladwin High School uniform, that kid starts following me everywhere. He asks me to go see *Lethal Weapon*, and to Nelson Park to feed the deer after school, and to Jon's Drive-In for a burger and fries, and after a while I sort of get used to him. He even gives me his varsity ring one night, all silver and sparkly with a ruby in the center, and it is a real thrill to show up at school the next day and show it off to everyone, but no matter how much yarn I wrap around that thing, it just never seems to fit me quite right.

Sometime late in the season, when it's so cold that our bare legs go numb in our uniforms, those cheers start to feel like second nature. It's this one particular game where I realize it, when I'm standing on the sidelines doing *Cardinals! Cardinals! Fight, Fight, Fight!* and suddenly I don't even have to think about it. My hands and feet and voice are so in tune with those other cheerleaders that it's like we're one big body out there, and I feel safe, safe, safe, like I will belong forever and nobody can kick me out.

But then I notice Rosemary Fuller sitting up in the stands under a blanket with Wendell Biggs. Like they're on a *date* or something. And I really can't believe it. I can't believe Wendell is out with Rosemary. I can't believe Rosemary is out with anyone at all, and the worst part is how happy she looks. And I feel just awful about how much I hate them both right then, and how much I wish it was me up there with Wendell, and also how glad I am that it's not.

Then Wendell catches me watching them, and I don't know what to do, so I try to find my parents in the crowd. When I spot them, they're a few rows from the top with Grandma Mayzee right between them, and they wave and smile when they see me, like they're having a great time. But Mayzee just looks miserable, like she can't even figure out who *she* is anymore, and the whole time I'm out there jumping and rolling and shaking those pom-poms, I just can't help but feel so sorry for her. I mean, it must be terrible to forget who you are, just terrible.

Rebound

A year after you cancel your wedding to the playwright who calls you provincial because you don't like hanging out with his ex-girlfriends, you will realize it is time to break up with your new companion, who will start to annoy you after months of littering your apartment floor with ice cream sandwich wrappers and looming over you in bed each morning until you jump out of sleep with a start.

But in the weeks that follow the last conversation you will ever have with the playwright, a phone call about the guest list that lasts no more than twenty minutes, you can't imagine yourself with anyone but him. In the weeks that follow, you burn up two coffee pots, bounce seven checks, drive your car into a highway divider, set your hair on fire lighting a novena candle, and make it all the way to your car twice before you notice the groceries rattling loose in your cart and realize you forgot to bag-it-yourself, all because you can't stop the argument in your head where you say the clever, biting things you were too stunned to think of when he told you there was no point in marrying you unless Samantha, Carmen, Dahlia, Monique and Astrid could all be there to watch.

You explain it to people with a tight little smile, say it was all for the best, but knowing this is true doesn't help you one bit. You talk around him, about the church or the reception hall or the invitations, but can't say his name out loud and refuse to let anyone else, either, even the woman who takes your address when you call to order pizza.

"Building P as in Peter?" she asks.

"Building P," you say, "as in *pig*."

Everyone thinks they can help you get over your grief. Your mother tells you not to think about him and repeats phrases like "you need to let go of your anger." Your sister says she always thought he was gay. Your father promises that time heals all wounds and every cloud has a silver lining, and Sister Agnes Rita, who shares your office at the Catholic school where you teach, tells you that with God all things are possible. Even your doctor thinks he can help you, something you learn when you drive to the drugstore after calling him twice a day to complain about stomach aches and discover that what he's prescribed for you is Prozac.

One day your best friend calls up and says it's been six months and it's time to get back in the saddle, so you agree to have dinner with an engineer she knows who seems much less intellectual in the rib joint where he takes you than he did when he called to make plans. He tells stories about getting stoned with his football team in high school and you laugh until you cry at the one about his teammate who claimed to be surfing as he stood in the bowl of a toilet and flushed, but the whole time you're eating you can't help but feel a little guilty, and when the date is over, you get out of his car and think *I can't do this.*

Because as the beer in your refrigerator and the pork rinds in your pantry and the extra clothes in your closet all remind you, you've fallen into another relationship since you called off your wedding, one that began innocently enough over a bottle of wine after work, and progressed, in a traditional sort of way, to boxes of Belgian chocolates that became silk scarves that turned into expensive perfumes that led to strands of pearls that now fill your jewelry box and decorate the top of your dresser. You don't like to think of yourself as shallow – and in truth you've never been taken in by such tripe before – but after playing second fiddle to a bunch of ex-girlfriends, the charm of feeling like the only woman in the world was just impossible to resist.

And so, after months of insisting that, really, you were perfectly *fine*, that your job was all you needed to be happy and your cat was all the company you wanted, you tumbled into bed anyway, gasping and moaning in a storm of sheets and blankets after holding out for so long, and it was such a relief, because you knew it was sort of inevitable, though when you emerged from the bedroom three days later, you wondered if this made you as bad as your friend in college who gave up closing her curtains on her peeping tom and slept with him instead. *Persistence is seductive,* she'd shrugged the next morning, and now you understand what she meant, because ever since you finally gave in, you've been so consumed that you've just about given up answering the phone, or returning messages, or accepting invitations for parties and movies and gatherings at pubs the way you always complained your friends did when they got into serious relationships, though you can totally understand why they just wanted to stay in bed.

Maybe you aren't crazy about the fact that George Strait or Reba McIntyre always seem to be on in your apartment now, or that you're up pacing the slippery wood floors at night instead of sleeping because you haven't adjusted to all of the tossing and turning, all the sorting out of pillows, all the remapping of foot space at the end of the bed, but you love the jelly donuts that wait for you each morning on the kitchen counter, and appreciate not having to think about money, and can't help but marvel that you can be so open about your feelings without starting a fight when every ex-boyfriend you've ever had looked nervous if you so much as sniffled.

Of course, it's a different sort of life than the one you had with the playwright, like comparing apples to oranges, really, and you try not to let yourself think about the fact that you're not in love because the effortless routine you've slipped into works for you, mostly, so even if you're sometimes frustrated by the dirty glasses left around your apartment or the wet towels you find on the bathroom floor, at least you know exactly what to expect each day: the early-morning revel that makes you late for class, the reunion after work that leads you back under the covers, and then *David Letterman* instead of *The Tonight Show*, with no negotiation at all about which is funnier, until the credits roll and you head back to bed, only to wake up the next morning and do it all over again.

So the quarter-inch stubble and the shaggy, unwashed hair, the crumpled clothes and the scandalously inappropriate comments, even the drinking – these you overlook because everything is going along pretty smoothly otherwise, though it becomes harder to ignore the fact that they just don't fly as well in public at the faculty Christmas party, where things get off to a bad start when you show up late from an afternoon rendezvous that goes on far too long. There's a moment after you've arrived, just before the second martini, where it looks like maybe you've worried for nothing, like maybe things will be fine after all, but as the evening progresses, it becomes more and more difficult not to feel a little jealous that all of the other teacher's dates are so well-dressed and polite, and although everyone is perfectly nice about everything – a little too nice, you think – it's obvious that they're uncomfortable, and when you wake up the next morning wondering how it all must have looked, even you have to admit that this is just one of those things other people couldn't possibly understand.

One day you answer the phone for the first time in ages and it's your mother on the other end. She says she's worried about you and hands the phone to your father, who tells you that opportunity waits for no man and you need to make hay while the sun shines.

"A watched pot never boils," you say in his language.

But he only sighs and says, "Honey, it's time to let go."

You tell him that it's none of their business anyway, that it's your life and you'll live it your way, thank you very much, but after you've slammed down the receiver and taken a good look around you, it becomes harder to ignore the fact that maybe they're right, because little things you never noticed before have started to bother you, and you can't figure out how you missed them. As if Randy Travis and Loretta Lynn aren't bad enough, the smoking disgusts you, and you're tired of wading through the dirty clothes and soggy wads of Kleenex left just lying on your floor, and the fact that reruns of *American Gladiators* or *Three's Company* never seem to let up, something you could actually change except that you don't want to face the stony silence you know pressing "Off" on the remote will produce. And though you've known for a while that the drinking was a problem, your recent discovery that there are too many empty whiskey bottles hidden in your hall closet to retrieve your vacuum cleaner without risking your life means it's even worse than you initially thought.

Still, you think maybe it's just that you need to get out more often, so you accept an invitation to go see an Italian film with the girls one day after work, a story about a middle-aged woman who leaves her philandering husband and takes a job in Venice, but midway through the movie, in the dark of the theater, your face starts to feel a little funny and it takes you a moment to realize you are smiling. It's the first time you've been around your friends in so long, the first time you've watched anything but total trash in months, but any hope you might have about doing this more often is dashed when you are kept awake that night by noisy, drunken sobs and then startled by more when you finally fall asleep. *They're my friends*, you try reasoning in the morning, *I need to spend time with them*, but this only leads to so much wailing and nose-blowing that you flounce out of the bedroom and slam the bathroom door behind you.

In the mirror you notice the circles under your eyes, the sallowness of your skin, the general puffiness of your reflection because you can't find a single can of tuna or slice of bread in your pantry behind all those crappy pork rinds, and for a moment you wonder if you weren't better off with the playwright. But you knew when you cancelled the wedding that you couldn't have spent your life watching your husband hug and kiss his ex-girlfriends, telling them how wonderful they were, how beautiful, how much he loved them all. It was like watching a dog that can't stop humping people's legs. It made you sick to your stomach, and you knew, without knowing how, that he was doing it to hurt you, though you could never think of anything you might have done to make him angry.

You wanted something better, and you hoped this might be it, but what felt at first like safety now seems stifling somehow, though maybe it's just because you've grown bored with the bed-television-bed-television routine that never seems to vary except for what you eat: some nights it's potato chips, other nights, it's Twinkies. The truth is that you'd like to have a real dinner once in a while, preferably out, but there's just no getting anywhere with this line of thinking once the *Dukes of Hazzard* marathon starts and someone is a few Manhattans up on the night.

The whole thing is just too high maintenance to manage when you have term papers to grade and a cat that needs his litter changed and a father who keeps leaving messages on your answering machine asking just exactly what the Sam Hill is going on out there in Baltimore anyway, and so you decide to put an end to it in the way you always have, by staying late at work, accepting more invitations to go out with your friends, and taking the long walks you gave up at some point along the way, so that you won't have to admit the truth, which is that you're just tired and embarrassed and finally understand that, as your father keeps saying, it's time to let go.

But when the day finally comes that you slide your key into the lock after work and feel the stillness before you even push open the door, you think for a second that maybe this isn't what you wanted after all. You drop your keys and gloves and hat on the dining room table and look around, but only Mr. D'Arcy is there, flicking his tail back and forth, winding himself around your ankles. *What's the story, kid?* you ask him, but he only purrs and nudges you toward his empty bowl on the kitchen floor, and when you open up the refrigerator to get his can of food, you notice that the beer is gone too.

At first you are convinced that this really must be it, but for a while all it takes is a single sharp reminder – a song on the radio, a forgotten snapshot that drops out of a book – and before you even know how it's happened, there's a bucket of ice and a half-empty bottle of Maker's Mark on your coffee table, Travis Tritt and cigarette smoke in the air, and once or twice you even wind up in bed again. Even later, after these final bittersweet trysts lose their appeal, you sometimes get the feeling that you're being trailed through the stacks at the library or followed through the park, but you know from experience that if you just ignore stalkers, they usually give up.

When it's finally over there's nothing to mark it in any dramatic way, like in a romance novel where the heroine comes through a long ordeal and suddenly there's a man there waiting for her, the right man after the wrong man has nearly done her in, though one day you'll find yourself laughing in the passenger's seat of a car on a warm afternoon and the man driving will reach over and rest his hand above your knee and you'll put your hand on top of his and ride like that for miles, spring air and sunlight streaming through the windows, and no matter how hard you try, you won't be able to recall why you were ever so sad in the first place. But this doesn't happen right away.

What happens right away is that you notice that your head isn't pounding when you wake up anymore the way it did every morning for months, and when you teach and grocery shop and pick up your dry cleaning, people no longer knit their brows when they talk to you, looking puzzled or concerned or offended. In your shower, you discover that a pink razor with a fresh blade has replaced the one that had rusted to the ledge of the bathtub around Labor Day, and in your mailbox, you find, for the first time in almost a year, a credit card statement that does not shock the hell out of you. One evening you stop by the liquor store on your way to a dinner party, but at the register, the cashier does not call you by name or ask if you need cigarettes with the bottle of wine you buy, and when the night is over, none of the other guests insist that it would really be no trouble at all if you would just please hand over your keys, get into the goddamn car, and let them drive you home.

And then one balmy Tuesday late in March, after you've driven home from work and changed into your jeans, after you've fed Mr. D'Arcy and returned your father's calls, after you've put on Ella Fitzgerald and the streaks of pink have faded into stars out your living room windows pushed open to the breeze, you pick up the phone and order a pizza from a man who writes down what you want on it and asks for your address.

"It's Building *P*," you say, "as in *Peter*."

Overtime

When Carrie Sinclair arrived late to her son's game and scanned the bleachers in the packed high school gymnasium, the nearest available seat was the one right next to Pam Donnelly, the woman who, for seventeen years, Carrie had successfully managed to avoid. Which took some doing in a town as small as Cedar. Seventeen years of a different checkout lane at Giant, of an alternate entrance into the Broadway Movie Theater, of an elevator on the other end of the Davis Clinic from the department where Pam worked as a nurse. Seventeen years of practiced distraction, an expression that was some mixture of innocence and preoccupation that made it seem like you just weren't paying attention. You couldn't be accused of ignoring someone, Carrie had long ago discovered, if you got the look just right.

But for the past two months Carrie's son Jeffrey and Pam's son Billy had been playing on the same basketball team at the high school where Carrie and Pam had once been students themselves, and this development had presented Carrie with a whole new set of challenges that required a recalibration of her tactics. There were the daily practices where Carrie had learned to spot Pam's car in front of the school and make another lap around the block to avoid pulling up behind her, home games at which she'd taken to identifying Pam's coat on the bleachers even when Pam wasn't sitting there, out-of-town games where, in a pinch, she could identify Pam's shoes under the bathroom stall and head off to find a drinking fountain just to kill a few minutes, just to avoid running into Pam and having to make small talk at the sinks. And for two months it had worked. So Carrie didn't know whether it was forgiveness, or curiosity, or maybe just the energy she finally didn't have to climb up five more rows and topple over the Meyers, the Wilsons and the Pitts to get to the only other empty seat in the gym that made her finally plunk down next to Pam, and ask breezily, as though it were nothing, how the game was going.

"Good," Pam said, and if she was surprised, she didn't show it. In fact, when she spoke next it was with enthusiasm. "Too bad you missed it," she said. "Jeffrey just made a great shot." Jeffrey, Carrie's son. Hearing his name come out of Pam's mouth with such ease was stranger still. And Pam seemed perfectly comfortable, judging from her posture, perhaps even pleased, that Carrie had sat down next to her. But now it was Carrie's turn to speak, and she didn't know what to say. She didn't even know how to arrange her face after so many years of studied obliviousness to Pam's presence. So she checked the scoreboard, took a deep breath, and asked how Pam's son Billy had played – the boy whose very existence, if she thought about it too much, could still open up that old wound inside and make her bleed.

Back in high school, they'd been friendly, even sat together in these same old bleachers sometimes, because Carrie's boyfriend Jared and Pam's boyfriend Daryl had played on the same team back then, on the very court where Carrie and Pam now watched their sons play. But Jared had been the real star. He was skinny and small for a basketball player, not even six feet tall, and his height had forced him to hone techniques for sinking shots that would give him the best advantage – a layup in which he cut under the man covering him and popped up on the other side, a three-pointer from the corner that always went in, and when all else failed, a wild charge into the lane that often left him sprawled on the floor, accusing the defender, whose fault he claimed it was. He often fouled out of games.

But Carrie had been enthralled watching him play in those days. He had nerve, something Carrie, unfailingly polite and quiet, had always lacked, something she admired in Jared. He was outgoing and well-liked, even by teachers who sometimes gave him Ds and Fs on papers and exams, and was voted "Most Popular" on their senior mock elections. Carrie, on the other hand, had been voted "Most Likely To Succeed," a category that had seemed unexciting to her compared with "Most Beautiful" or "Most Outgoing" though together, Carrie and Jared had been voted "Most Likely To Get Married."

But in the end, they hadn't. Instead, Carrie had left for a university two hours away and Jared had stayed behind to attend community college, and one night on the phone, after a fight over something Carrie could no longer remember, they had broken up. They often did this: Jared would forget to call, or wouldn't show up on a weekend he'd promised to visit, or forget to send a letter he'd promised to write, and after a long-distance argument, Carrie would slam the phone down, then wait until Jared showed up on her doorstep a week later, leaning on the doorjam of her room, sheepish and drunk, begging her to take him back. Until that week near the end of her sophomore year, when he suddenly didn't. One week had turned into two, then three, and several months passed before Carrie heard that Jared had up and married Pam. It wasn't until Billy was born six months later that she finally understood why Jared had never come.

Carrie had seen him only one time since, on her first day of the summer job she'd picked up at the Burger Barn back in Cedar while she looked for a real job, and where Jared had materialized one afternoon with Billy on his hip. His eyes had been fixed on the menu posted on the window, and he'd already begun reading off his order when he realized it was Carrie behind the screen. He'd paused for a second, looking at her levelly in a way that made her heart hammer under her tee shirt, then averted his eyes, and asked how she was doing. She pretended to focus on mixing his milkshake and answered coolly that she'd graduated in May.

He didn't congratulate her, which was okay, since she couldn't bring herself to congratulate him either, on the marriage or the child, and in any case he didn't look like he wanted congratulations: he seemed older, and tired, had even lost a bit of his hair. But something else was different. He looked, Carrie thought, like he was about to bolt – and when he really did skip town a few months later, leaving Pam alone to raise Billy, Carrie thought of Billy's little hand reaching for the kiddie cone she'd made for him that day, how he'd giggled when she handed it to him, then buried his face in the flimsy sleeve of Jared's shirt.

In the years that followed, Carrie often reminded herself she was lucky: it could have been *her* Jared Fussman had skipped out on after all, leaving her with a child to raise. But instead, Carrie Buchanan became not Carrie *Fussman*, as she'd expected, but Carrie *Sinclair* when she'd married Richard, who had appeared at her window at the Burger Barn that same summer, and kept appearing, ordering increasingly elaborate sandwiches so that he could spend the extra time it took Carrie to assemble them asking her about college and who she'd seen from high school and what her future plans were. Richard, who had graduated two years before she had from Cedar High, who'd become a CPA at a firm thirty miles west of town, in Lansing. Richard, who had given Carrie their son Jeffrey and a house in Briar Woods that she'd never dared dream about as a child. Besides being handsome and funny, Richard was compulsively punctual, never drank more than two beers, put the toilet seat down, even helped out in the kitchen sometimes. And whenever Carrie thought about the path that had led her to him, she felt like the universe had made a decision for her that was infinitely better than the one she'd have made for herself at twenty, given the choice.

But at other times, when the sunlight was angled just so, and the daffodils were giving way to the tulips, and spring was unseasonably warm, she remembered the night during sophomore year when, after months of eye-batting and note passing and rumors, Jared had offered to walk her home after a baseball game and stopped to press her into the ladder of the monkey bars at the playground they'd passed along the way, where he'd buried his face in her hair and confessed that he'd loved her since they were children, and Carrie had known right then and there that Jared would become her entire world.

It was as if her humdrum existence in a town nobody had ever heard of suddenly blossomed into something glorious and sprawling, epic and meaningful – *someone loved her!* – and it was a meaning she'd never questioned, even after Jared's drinking got worse and she started catching him in little lies. And even later, after Jared had abandoned Pam and Billy, Carrie still believed sometimes that Jared would have been different with her. Perhaps he wouldn't have felt the need to bolt, because they'd have only had children when they were ready. Perhaps he'd never really loved Pam the way he'd loved Carrie, never buried his face in Pam's hair like he couldn't ever get enough of her smell and told her he'd loved her all his life.

Mostly, though, she didn't think about it. She loved Richard, was happy in her life with him, and Jeffrey was, on the whole, a joy. Even at 14, in the throes of adolescence, he seemed to take the whole thing in stride. Just last week his voice had cracked while he answered the phone, an awkward "Hel-*lo?*" that sent Richard and Carrie into gales of laughter, but he was such a good sport about it all, shaking his head and handing off the phone to Richard with a look that seemed to say, "Oh, well." And so life hummed along, except on those days when Carrie's path happened to cross Pam's and that old feeling of not having measured up to Pam in some way would wash over her like a cloud passing over the sun, and she would have to be firm with herself, remind herself that she was a good wife and mother, that though she had never lived up to her "Most Likely to Succeed" billing, she was a good colleague at the bank where she worked as a manager, and that at 38, she was (Richard said, anyway) still attractive. But even then sometimes that old hangdog feeling would trail her until a smile from Richard or a joke from Jeffrey returned her to her usually peaceful frame of mind.

And now, sitting next to Pam in the bleachers after all this time, she felt that old question bubbling up again, a question she'd never been able to ask Jared, a question that had plagued her for years: What *was* it about Pam that had made Jared finally throw it all away? A few years ago when her old friend Carly had been in town for the holidays and they'd met for burgers at the Pixie Diner, Carrie had confessed, not for the first time, that she still wondered about this, and Carly had simply shaken her head, taken Carrie's hands across the table, and said, "He was a twenty-year-old *boy* and Pam was *there*. End of story. Will you give this up already?" And because Pam *had* been pretty, and because Carly had always been so sensible and worldly – she'd graduated from college too, taken a job in Cleveland, and fled Michigan for good – Carrie said, "Yes. I will give it up." And she had never mentioned Jared again, to anybody.

But with Pam beside her now, Carrie couldn't help noticing

that Pam's skin showed signs of old scars from acne Carrie didn't remember her ever having. What Carrie remembered was her own acne, those little bumps she spent hours trying to conceal before school, praying the makeup would stay on all day. Carrie also remembered Pam's hair as long and dark and smooth compared to Carrie's own wispy blonde tufts that she was constantly trying to thicken with hairspray and a blowdryer, but up close she noticed Pam's hair was actually rough in texture, that it looked, in fact, like it hadn't been brushed in a week, and now Carrie couldn't remember if this was how Pam had always looked or if this was a result of the struggle Carrie knew too well herself: to be a mother and hold down a job and keep up with the needs of children and husbands and bosses. Because after Jared had skipped out on her, Pam had married Daryl Donnelly after all, the high school boyfriend who had adopted Billy, but who worked out of town like Carrie's own husband Richard, and so rarely made it to a game.

At one point, while Carrie was examining Pam's teeth – which were not the straight white pearls of a toothpaste commercial she recalled, but in fact, a bit stained and uneven – Pam seemed to sense Carrie's eyes upon her, and – as if she thought Carrie wanted to ask her a question – turned to let her ask it. But the question Carrie wanted to ask was one Pam couldn't answer, and, flushed with shame, Carrie fled the gym with Jeffrey in tow when the game was over, vowing she'd never sit next to Pam Donnelly again.

But she had, mainly because when she arrived at the gym for Jeffrey's game a week later, Pam was waving to her from the bleachers, so that Carrie could not possibly have taken the seat next to the Smiths, or the one beside the Wilsons. Instead, she had to climb up seven extra rows and topple over the Morgans to reach the seat Pam had saved for her. And Pam seemed genuinely happy to see her, something Carrie could not understand. It was as if the woman had no recollection of their shared history with a man who had altered the course of both of their lives forever, as if he was ancient history to her, as he should have been to Carrie, but for some reason, still wasn't.

And the truth was that sitting next to Pam that first night and finding nothing on the surface that would explain why Jared had chosen her all those years ago had only made Carrie even more curious about her, so that each successive game – where Pam began regularly saving Carrie a seat – only gave Carrie another opportunity to study Pam more closely. But the things she often noticed confused her even more. At one game, Pam cursed at a call the referee made, so crudely that it startled Carrie, who looked around to make sure no one else had heard. At another, she noticed that Pam chewed gum (gum! at her age!), blowing bubbles when the game got slow. Once, after an especially close game which Cedar had finally won, Pam even suggested they grab a bite to eat in celebration, so they drove the boys to the Pixie and piled into a booth, where Carrie took note of what Pam ordered – a double cheeseburger and large fries – and how she ate – big bites that left ketchup on the corners of her mouth, which Billy had to remind her to wipe away. And when she belched at the end of the meal, Carrie was so desperate for something that might suggest what Jared had seen in Pam all those years ago that when Pam opened her purse to dig around for her wallet, Carrie caught herself peeking inside, as if the answer to her question might be in there among Pam's keys and chapstick and little packets of kleenex.

As the season progressed, Carrie had to admit that it was hard not to like someone who seemed to like you so much, who lit up when you walked into a room and seemed to have been waiting *forever*

for you to appear. Then, too, Pam was always making wisecracks about Coach Daniels ("He'll never be a secret agent," she said after a freshman on the opposing team had seen Cedar's trick play coming a mile away) or even about her son Billy, who was prone to technical fouls ("He's really a nice kid," she'd said when Billy had thrown an elbow at the opposing team's point guard, "But not too bright."). And at times like these, Carrie remembered how funny Pam had always been, how she had always managed to be the center of attention back in high school, cracking up even the teachers who were trying to discipline her or doing keg stands at parties the kids always held deep in the woods, far from the prying eyes of the local cop.

Once, Carrie and Jared had even given Pam and Daryl a ride home from one of these parties, and the silence Pam left behind after they'd dropped her off made Carrie feel uptight and prudish, like she ought to loosen up a little, though she didn't really like the taste of beer, nor the feeling it gave her, and in truth, whenever her turn at the tap came, she always found a reason to be deep in conversation with Carly, or searching for something in the glove compartment of Jared's Jeep. But when she mentioned this to Jared, he'd said it was the fact that she *wasn't* like Pam that made her so special, didn't she know that? And, because she'd wanted to, Carrie had believed him.

But now, sitting next to Pam each week, she couldn't help but wonder: Had Jared been lying? Had she been wrong to believe him? Was it Pam that Jared had wanted all along?

Over the course of the two years their boys played basketball together, Carrie came to understand that she would never really know for sure what it was about Pam that had cost her the life she'd wanted so badly as a girl. It was one of those mysteries in life you just had to accept, she decided, like socks disappearing in the dryer or the new green leaves that sometimes grow from the dead branch of a tree. And it was then that the two women became friends again, meeting their husbands for supper at The Embers, or for dinner at one another's houses, the boys shooting hoops in the driveway at Carrie's or playing videogames in the basement at Pam's while the adults sat around the table drinking coffee and reminiscing about the year the old basketball team had almost won the state championship, or laughing about the cafeteria monitor who'd once put Daryl in detention for standing on a lunch table to pass a football to Scottie Gibbons. Often these memories included Jared tangentially – he'd been a member of the old team, after all, and played a part in most of the antics Daryl had instigated – but Pam and Daryl never mentioned Jared's name directly, and in all the time they spent together, Carrie never once asked about him.

But at one of the boys' very last games together, after Billy had flung himself into the midst of a fight that had broken out on the floor during overtime and was ejected from the game, Pam made the rueful observation that Billy was just like his father – "More balls than brains," is what she said – and after a moment she turned to Carrie and asked, "What on earth did you ever see in that guy?"

It seemed to Carrie that the gym got very quiet, and she was careful to keep her voice even when she said, "Oh, you know. I was young."

"Even so," Pam pressed. "You were with him for years."

"Well," Carrie asked, her heartbeat in her throat now. "What did *you* see in him?"

"That's easy," Pam said. "I figured if he was good enough for the great Carrie Buchanan, I was lucky he paid me any mind." She turned to Carrie and said, "You were always just so perfect, you know." Then Pam gazed out over the court, sighing deeply, almost wistfully, almost as if it were Carrie and not Jared she'd been missing all these years.

The Drill

Ethel's scrubbing potatoes for a salad in the kitchen and stewing about the fact that Vernon always forgets to thank her for her cooking or the time it takes to iron his pleated khakis or the way she's kept the floors clean for fifty years, until she drops the potatoes into a pot and sets them on the stove, and it's then that she notices he *still* hasn't fixed that front left burner she reminded him of on her way out to buy groceries for supper.

"Vernon," she calls to him in the next room, but the television is on and he doesn't answer.

"Vernon!" she shouts. Still no answer.

"Vernon?" she asks. And suddenly, standing there with a dish towel in one hand and a lid in the other, Ethel understands this is the moment she's been dreading. She heard the stories at Vernon's father's funeral: how his mother found his father slumped over his desk, how his grandmother spotted his grandfather keeled over in the snow, how his great-grandmother discovered his great-grandfather face-down by the woodpile. A history of women stumbling upon husbands who were supposed to be doing one thing but had up and died instead, and it is because of these stories that Ethel knows the drill.

In a flash she sees it all play out – how she'll step into the living room and find Vernon unnaturally still, remote in hand, how she'll check his pulse, her breathing coming hard and fast, how she'll dial

911 with a shaking hand and try to administer CPR to the beat she learned – *staying alive! staying alive!* – until the paramedics rush through the door and try to revive him, their big hands pumping, paddles at the ready. Then she'll huddle over his body because damned if they're going to carry him out of the house while he still looks like himself instead of the mess the morticians always make of even the best-looking folks, which Vernon isn't. Wasn't.

Next she'll make calls – to their children, his siblings, his mother, still kicking at 95. Then she'll head down to the Martin & Son Funeral Home and talk to the director over a big mahogany desk. He'll speak to her in soft tones, all business, as she picks out a casket, hymns, a flyer for the service. She'll hand over a picture of Vernon for the cover, snapped by their daughter on a recent trip to Cleveland. In it he will be smiling and alive, and she'll want the director to notice how nice his dentures are, but the director will be focused on other things. Terrible things: Which suit to bury him in? Which tie, socks, shoes? Does she want to keep his wedding band?

And the services, a day or two later: Ethel will choose dresses, one for the viewing, another for the funeral, put on the makeup she normally wears, though she'll fear people will say that she doesn't get it, that she's in shock, that she didn't really love him, because how could she care about mascara at a time like this? At the viewing she'll stand next to the shell of Vernon in his box, shrunken and plastic and expressionless while everyone, absolutely everyone, murmurs utterly useless things: *I know how you feel* or *It just takes time* and she'll think they're insensitive and clueless and flip, but she'll keep it to herself because she needs these people now, silly as they are, and in the end she'll be fine about the makeup because she can't seem to cry anyway and also because Buddy Harrington, who lost his wife three months ago, will show up for the funeral, and she'll be glad she doesn't look terrible in front of the boy who still pines for her after fifty years, though she'll wonder if this gladness makes her a horrible person.

Later, she'll sit beside the hole in the ground at the cemetery while the minister rambles. Ethel will know she should feel something meaningful in his words, and she'll nod along like she's listening, but instead she'll be remembering the Saturday morning she and Vernon chose this very plot together. They were in their thirties then and death seemed so far away and they felt very forward-thinking about it all, but what had seemed most real that day was the warm sunshine that filtered through the branches of the birches and turned the long rows of tombstones into something like a pretty park, and how the stroll through the cemetery had made them feel more urgent and aware and alive, how they seized on it that afternoon while the kids were at a picnic.

But after the undertakers lower Vernon's casket into the ground, after the handful of dirt filters through her fingers onto the domed hood that will seem far too shiny, after the reception her sister holds with three kinds of noodle casseroles and she's seen the last of her children off to their various flights and lives and jobs, she'll drive home and discover the house quiet in a way she never knew it could be. She'll understand then how another person gives off a low-level hum, even dozing three rooms away, and she'll wonder if it's like that *60 Minutes* segment she watched with Vernon about sounds the ear doesn't register but the brain detects, like those silent dog whistles or the tones only children can hear.

There will be clues that Vernon lived here once: his golf shirts hanging in the closet, his loafers kicked off in a corner of the den, his toothbrush where he left it on the bathroom counter the morning before he died. There will be the unmade bed where they slept their last night together, which Ethel will leave unmade for months while she sleeps on the couch because she can't bear the thought of disturbing those last traces of his existence. On days when she starts to go a little crazy, starts to wonder if he was ever alive or if she only imagined him that way, she will bury her face in his pillow just to smell his shampoo and shaving cream and sweat, his scent growing fainter all the time.

Bills that used to magically disappear will pile up on the dining room table. The checkbook won't ever be balanced. Garbage won't vanish from the kitchen when the trash is full, and it won't move from behind the garage to the curb by itself on trash day, either. The disposal will clog and she won't know how to fix it, and when the basement floods, not only will she not know where to rent a sump pump, she won't even know she needs one.

And the thing that will torture Ethel most as she lies sleepless on the couch each night, the one thing she won't be able to bear, are all of these little tasks of Vernon's that went unthanked, and the knowledge that she was more ungrateful than he was, but since he's not there to apologize to, he's not there to argue this point either, so sometimes she'll pretend they were both equally ungrateful for each other, or that maybe he was even a little more ungrateful than she was, and these are the only nights she'll ever fall asleep.

But there will always be more reminders: leaves she'll have to rake and bag, snow she'll have to shovel, which probably would have killed him anyway, she'll think, but when her lower back goes out and she's laid up for a week, she'll imagine him bursting in from outside, rosy and cheerful, the flakes still unmelted on his hat, asking *What's for lunch?* Sometimes this question could make her feel like the hired help, but if he were here now, she'll think, she'd fix him a sandwich on a big soft roll with extra turkey and crisp lettuce and slices of juicy tomato, a giant mound of the potato salad that was his final request on the side, and she'd do it, she knows, with a full and grateful heart.

With spring will come even more reminders: birds to keep from nesting in the eves, bats to chase from the attic, the lawn to cut, green and fresh and growing. And it's then that Buddy Harrington will happen by on a Sunday afternoon while Ethel is trying to get the hang of the weed whacker, so she'll let him rev the lawn mower to life, and when he's finished mowing she'll bring him the glass of lemonade she'd have brought Vernon every time if she'd been a better wife, and they'll sit together on the porch and talk about how no one should have to live alone, and a few weeks later she'll marry him in a civil ceremony down at the county courthouse.

෴

She's on her honeymoon with Buddy in Pensacola, an umbrella-topped cocktail in her hand, staring out at the green waves crashing on the white sand when she hears Vernon let out a yawn in the living room.

"Did you call me?" he asks, and Ethel takes a deep breath. She holds it in, lets it out. This is the fourth time he's done this to her in a month.

"You deaf old man," she scolds. "Why didn't you fix this stove?"

Boston Cream Pie

It's August when my friend Noelle calls to invite me to a barbecue. If she weren't the nicest person I know, she'd be the kind of woman I could easily hate: unwavering convictions, sparkling floors, outfits that work with her upswept hair – the kind of woman I spent the last two years trying to be, the kind of woman my ex-boyfriend Philip would have married. But I kept giving long answers to short questions and missing the dust bunnies under our couch and ending up in the jeans I'm always most comfortable wearing, my curls so wild that a layer of cement couldn't smooth them out for long, though that never stopped me from trying when we were together. And even if I finally understand that there's nothing more lonely than being loved for what you're only pretending to be, it's been four months and I still haven't forgiven myself because I'm not someone breezier, someone tidier, someone else.

Since the classes I teach let out in June I've spent the summer hiding from the Baltimore heat in my new studio apartment with the blinds drawn, talking only to the teenager who delivers my take-out and the cashiers at the Foodway on the corner of Gittings and Lake. So when I pick up the phone on a Sunday and find Noelle on the other end, it takes me a minute to answer about the barbecue – my people skills have decayed that much.

"Great," she says when I accept her invitation, and I'm still adjusting to the idea of actually socializing again when she adds: "How do you feel about being set up?"

Before I can tell her that I have a policy against blind dates because I don't relish the prospect of people I know looking on like spectators while the whole thing goes up in flames, she tells me a little about him: a teacher like me at a nearby school, mid-thirties, an old colleague from her former job. "He's really nice," she promises. "What do you think?"

What I think is, *Definitely not.* What I think is, *I'm not ready.*

Which is why I am surprised when what I say is that I'd like to meet him.

"I'll invite him to the barbeque," she tells me, and then our talk turns to her children, to the deadlines bearing down on us, to the summer that is dwindling to a close.

"One last thing," she says as we're getting off the phone. "Can you bring a dessert?"

I decide I'll bake my favorite kind of cake even though I never have before, and don't really know how. But on the day of the barbecue, I dig out the dusty copy of *The Joy of Cooking* my mother gave me when I first moved in with Philip, make a list, and head off to the store. I buy flour, sugar, butter, vanilla, cocoa and milk, but when I get home it turns out that I'm missing one of the eggs I was sure I had left in my refrigerator. There's only one in the carton when I open it up, a medium-sized one at that, so I crack it into the bowl, mix up the batter, pop it in the oven, and hope for the best, but when I check the filling I left bubbling on the stovetop, it turns lumpy in front of my eyes, and to make matters worse, when the cake comes out of the oven and I try to slice it open, the top half splits right down the middle.

Only the icing turns out, creamy and glossy and smooth. I

spread it on evenly, fill in the crack, notice the time, and go to work on myself, but it's roughly the same as baking the cake: the skirt I thought of wearing is balled up in the hamper, my lipstick is missing, and I'm not in the car five minutes when my hair starts to frizz. By the time I pull into Noelle's driveway the top layer of the cake is skewed to one side from the sharp left I took because I never see her street until it's almost too late, and when I look down to check my clothes before pressing the doorbell I discover that I'm wearing two different sandals – one navy and one brown, which looked identical back in my shadowy apartment but couldn't look more distinct here in the early evening light.

Noelle answers the door in a crisp yellow sundress that makes her skin glow.

"He's here," she whispers.

I recognize him across the crowded living room when I step inside. He's tall and skinny like Noelle described, with scruffy brown hair that falls over the top of his wire-rimmed glasses, and when he sees me standing there he comes right up and says hello. "I'm James," he tells me. "Annie," I say, and when I shake the hand he's extended, it's warm and strong and gentle. We seem to be off to a good start when he offers to bring me a drink, but when he returns with my Chardonnay, we stand off to the side of the room exchanging bits of information so bland that we might as well be filling out forms at the doctor's office: I was born in Rhode Island, teach history, and live on Charles Street. He was born in Wisconsin, teaches English, and lives on York Road – a dangerous part of Baltimore. I wonder out loud if he's ever been mugged.

"Almost," he tells me, and when I ask what he used to protect himself, he says, "Bad grammar." He says he used to live in Roland Park when he worked in computers, but he got tired of spending all day talking about things that didn't really matter. "Do you know what I mean?" he asks in a way that doesn't require an answer, but I do know what he means because I left my job writing insurance manuals for the exact same reason, and I'm just about to say this when out of nowhere two children crash into us fighting over a doll. The air is pierced by sudden sobs, followed by the sympathetic laughter of the adults who make jokes about sibling rivalry. "It's not just kids," Noelle observes. "My sister's an adult but she's still evil," and people around the room jump right in after her: everyone, it seems, has an "evil sibling."

When James offers an awkward, "I have four siblings but none of them are evil," I worry for a second that what Noelle meant when she said he was *really nice* is that he's really boring. Then he says, "Maybe that means *I'm* the evil sibling," and it's as if a light comes on inside me. Even after I've stopped laughing, I can feel something warm beneath my rib cage, a kind of surge that runs all the way down to my knees, and by the time James brings up his yellow lab named Rodney, I'm flushed and damp and have to remind myself to calm down, which is easier to do when I realize that he's staring at my shoes.

At the dinner table Noelle seats us right next to each other and I try to think of something to say about myself that will impress him, but when our conversation turns to our families I accidentally mention that my grandmother spent seven years in a mental institution, and when he asks if insanity runs in my family I tell him it's supposed to skip a generation before I even realize what I've said. Then I drop a chicken wing into my lap, and I can already hear my phone not ringing as I try to wipe barbecue sauce off my shirt and only succeed in smearing it around even more, but when I look up again, James is smiling at me. It's a smile I can't quite read, but a smile nonetheless, and I let myself wonder what it means all the way through another chicken wing, some Waldorf salad and a roll, until a silky brunette across the table mentions that she's a Packers fan and James jerks his head up so fast even I get whiplash. "No kidding," he says, and I eat two more rolls right then and there because not only am I not a Packers fan, but I'm not even sure what they play, and by the time James has finished talking sports, the dinner is over and I'm just waiting to slink out to my car and escape into the night.

But there's still dessert to get through. Noelle directs us to a side table with fresh plates and forks and the two desserts she says we can choose between: on the one side, a crystal bowl she's filled with chocolate trifle, fresh raspberries and mint leaves that looks like a cover for *Good Housekeeping*, and on the other side, my cake. In line, James stands so close to me that his shoulder brushes mine, but the flicker of hope I feel as we wait fizzles out when I notice that Noelle's dessert is halfway gone while mine still sits untouched by the other guests. I can't really take it personally – little beads of condensation have broken out on the icing now and the whole thing looks like it's caving in on itself. Even I'm angling for some of Noelle's trifle, just waiting for James to ladle his up with the serving spoon before I reach for some. But he doesn't move. He's looking at my cake, and when I realize this it suddenly feels like it's me he's appraising: a lumpy, lopsided, broken, crumbling, sinking, sweaty mess.

He cuts himself an enormous slice.

Chasing the Sun

It's raining in the parking lot when I first arrive. *The drop point*, it was called in the flyer that advertised this trip, and so I pull out my umbrella as other cars unload and drive away. Clouds loom over Table Mountain in the distance, and beneath it Cape Town looks grainy and gray. We make awkward introductions as we wait for the truck to arrive, but the others all speak languages I don't understand, which, for once, is fine with me. I'm wounded and wary anyway, and not looking to make any new friends.

When the truck pulls up, we stow our backpacks in the bins above our seats and head for our first campsite, where our guide Pieter runs through the rules: for the next two months, we will eat only what he tells us to, drink only water from the truck, will not so much as brush our teeth in tap water once we hit Namibia. "Unless you want worms," he says, in case it isn't clear. Pieter is wiry and blonde with a tan so deep it must reach his bones, and though his accent says he hails from Johannesburg, I can't imagine him in the city, or as a child. He seems to have materialized fully formed out of the dry desert air, and his whole bearing tells us he understands this place in a way the rest of us never will as he rattles off ways to keep jackals out of our tents: no food, no wine, no unzipped flaps.

I fled the United States six months ago to study in South Africa, or at least that's the official reason I gave when anyone asked why I left. The unofficial reason is that my heart got broken, and for a solid year I could only think of Michigan as the state where my heart got broken, my hometown as the city where my heart got broken, the Burger King on the corner of Mission and Broomfield as the place I hung out after the bars closed with the man who broke my heart. So I ended up in Cape Town, where I walked the gardens outside Parliament, buried my face in *feinbos*, ate *boerveors*, pet zebras, danced with street musicians, and drank in shebeens, and just about the time I was starting to forget him, an American student convinced me to ditch class to hike up Table Mountain with him, and by the time we hiked down eight hours later, Table Bay and the city shimmering beneath us, I was in love again.

Two months later it was Cape Town I needed to escape: The Obs Café where we studied, The Rolling Stone where we drank, the mountain we hiked every weekend until he left, something you can't ever help seeing in Cape Town because it towers over the city like a protective giant, there every time you look up. I put him on a plane home when classes let out for the summer, feeling shattered and stupid for letting myself get involved yet again, and the next day, walking along the Main Road, I tore down a flyer from a company advertising overland trips to Victoria Falls and walked down to their office to sign up.

I imagine this trip will be my escape from my escape: I'll know no one on the trip, will move through territories that hold no memories, places more occupied by elephants and zebra than people, everything solemn and solitary, I think, the sound track from "Out of Africa" playing in the background. And emerging from my tent in Clanwilliam after our first night of the trip, the

Cederberg Mountains are so purple in the early morning silence that I think, yes, *this* will help me let go, *this* will help me forget.

But as we head for the Namibian border, Pieter blasts Janis Joplin from the cab of the truck and my Dutch seatmate Hans tries to engage me with what I'm dismayed to discover is decent English, and after a stop at a vineyard on our way out of town, everyone around me gets friendly, then tipsy, then drunk. Two hours later they've all passed out except for my assigned tentmate, Christo, a Greek student, who is just drunk enough to ignore all of Pieter's warnings to be unfailingly polite at the border, so we sit for three hours while the officer eats dinner, smokes a cigarette, and finally opens the gate. By the time we reach our campsite on the Orange River, Christo is unconscious on the backseat of the truck, his mouth hanging open, so I struggle with the clumsy poles of our tent by myself, and feel grateful without wanting to when Hans appears beside me to help.

The next morning we head off for a hike along the curlicues of rock outcroppings, the others talking and laughing while I trail behind on my own, and the next day I opt out of the canoe trip down the Orange River just to get a break from their chatter. They return hours later, sunburned and chummy in ways I don't trust because in two months we'll never see each other again, and I feel smug and self-satisfied because I won't be the one hurting when this is all over, so after a supper of *boervoers* cooked over the fire, I wash up in the last bathroom we'll see for a week and head off to bed, passing the group, who've moved on to gin and tonics around the campfire. Hans smiles at me as I pass, as if to say I'm welcome too, but I smile back tightly and crawl into my tent, wondering why it didn't occur to me how many people I'd have to avoid on this trip, wondering how on earth I'm going to make it all the way to Victoria Falls. But one afternoon just before we hit Swakopmund, Pieter pulls the truck over and tells us to get out in the hundred degree heat and walk in different directions for an hour, just so we can spend some time completely alone in the desert, and I think *finally* as I head south until I can no longer see the truck or the others behind the gentle dips of the landscape.

Namibia is a country where you can drive the four days it has taken us to get here without seeing a town, a rest stop, a single other car. And now, in the midst of its red-baked earth that stretches around me as I follow Pieter's directions to keep walking for an hour, I've never seen so much sky, all the way to the horizon in every direction, and I can't believe that in such uninterrupted vastness there could be no wind. But with only the ground below me, the sky above me, the incredible silence that surrounds me, I finally have what I came for: true solitude, complete desolation.

But after only half an hour of walking, I begin to feel a little uneasy. My water bottle is half empty but my mouth is dry again, and as far as I can see there is no rocky crag, no tree, no scrubby brush to offer me shade from the sun. I still can't see the truck or any of the others, and suddenly I wonder if I'm disoriented. I look behind me to see if my footprints are there to guide me back to the truck, but when I do, there's no sign I've ever been here: the earth is so dry that my shoes haven't made a dent. I think, *What if I'm lost out here? What if I can't find my way back?* And though I'm supposed to keep going for another half hour, I turn back suddenly, something like terror propelling me, and when I finally emerge from a dip in the landscape twenty minutes later and see some of the others waving to me through the shimmering heat, I'm flooded with joy I don't expect to feel and approach them with gladness. Hans extends his skinny arm to me when I reach the truck and pulls me up onto the roof beside him, where I take sips of the "wodka" he offers me from the flask he keeps in his pocket and we wait for the rest of the group to come in.

The next morning, I don't lag so far behind on our hike up the Sossusvlei Dunes, blood-red and undulating to the horizon, and on our way out of Swakopmund, I catch myself laughing as Hans sings along to "California Dreaming" in his broken English. I even join the group around the campfire the next night, accepting the gin and tonic my tentmate Christo fixes me without asking, and the coat the beautiful Danish girl Vibeka offers when the desert turns suddenly cold around dusk. Another night I let the Welsh girl Cass put little braids in my hair when she asks, and the next morning the Belgian banker Tomas lends me his sunblock as we hike into Fish River Canyon, where he sweats profusely and finally retches from the heat. When we reach the bottom he eases himself into the water and bobs with his eyes closed while I dive in fully-clothed with the others and swim until it's time to hike out again, though I stick close to Tomas on the trail, letting him drink my extra water when his bottle runs dry.

I'm getting used to them all, I realize, even take comfort in their presence after my scare in the desert, though it's an impersonal comfort, the kind neighbors you don't really know in the apartment next door offer when something goes bump in the night. Then one afternoon, a crisis: We've been on the road for hours, our campsite half a day behind us, when Vibeka starts ransacking her bags in the seat in front of me, speaking frantic Danish. "What is it?" I ask. "What has happened?" And her fingers fly and grasp and tear as she searches, as she tries to explain to me, in the little English she knows, what is wrong. "A talisman," she says, "an elephant." And though I am not sure exactly what this means, I know she is heartbroken as she finally gives up searching and sinks into her seat sobbing, not bothering to hide her grief, and I know that what she has lost is something dear to her, something irreplaceable that is gone forever. When her sobs subside she sits slumped in resignation, and it is then that Tomas leans across the aisle and admits he is here because of a woman, a French girl who left him back in Brussels, he says, and that's when I admit why I'm here, too: *a man*, I say. And though Hans does not add anything, I understand by then that medical school has stolen from him any chance of a normal life, his loneliness as heavy a burden as his giant suitcase that Pieter stows on the roof of the truck because it is too large to fit into the overhead bin.

And yet, in spite of knowing these things, I still try to keep my distance from everyone, still go to bed hours before the others, though each morning I find myself increasingly curious about what I missed. Sometimes I can put two and two together, if Christo's sleeping bag is empty beside me in the morning and then I see him emerge from the flap of Cass's tent, or if there are gin bottles smashed by the fire and I have to help Pieter wake the others up. But other times, these same clues leave me mystified: one very early morning while camped at the foot of the Spitzkoppe I awake beside a woman I don't recognize who turns out to be Christo wearing lipstick and a pair of Vibeka's stilettos, and when I crawl out of the tent I see Pieter pouring coffee for Tomas, who is sporting Cass's sundress.

As the days pass, I cannot help but acknowledge that I have come to know these people in spite of not wanting to: the way Vibeka shakes her yellow hair when she emerges from her tent each morning; the way Hans's eyes are watchful as we careen through the desert except when they droop and finally close at 3:00 each afternoon; the way that Tomas's face will bloom like a time-lapsed flower when he discovers a beetle the size of a fist he can leave on Vibeka's seat, and the way Vibeka will shriek when she finds it. And though Cass swears every night that she's not drinking, that last night was it, forever, no more, I know the way she'll stagger out of her tent in the morning, flop face down on the blanket where Pieter makes breakfast, half wailing, half whispering: "I'm wrecked." I know, too, the way Pieter will smile at her then, how he will poke her with the toe of his sandal and say it's no worse than she deserves, but after a while he will kneel next to her like a doctor over his patient, administering coffee fixed the way she likes it: lots of sugar, no milk.

And despite all of my efforts to prevent it, I can't deny that these people know me too when I discover a sketch they left of our group on the paper tablecloth of a bar in Maun. The stick-figure me is sitting in the back seat of the truck next to the stick-figure Hans with a bubble coming out of my mouth that says *Oh my God!* and it takes me just seconds to realize that they're right: *everything* surprises me. But it is the strokes they've used to draw me that make me like myself better in that moment than I have or will for years to come: I'm waving wildly and smiling, my elbow thrown out exuberantly, my ball cap drawn at a jaunty angle.

At the last campsite in Namibia, just before we cross the border into Botswana, I strip down with the others and we dive into the Kavango river at sunset, drunk and laughing, and swim across the border to Angola, wandering among the wildflowers and the cows in the meadow beyond which we dare not venture for fear of land mines, so we swim back, exhausted and exhilarated, and collapse on Pieter's blanket until the embers of the campfire die and the stars emerge above us, bright as jewels. When I say how many there are, more than I've ever seen, Pieter reminds us how unremarkable our own sun is, just a smallish star, he says, just a speck in the universe, and I want to stay right here at this exact moment forever, my head on Hans's shoulder, Cass's feet propped up against mine, Christo mixing gin and tonics beside me as Pieter points out Centaurus and Sagittarius and the Southern Cross.

In the years to come I will pinpoint this as the exact moment I gave in to belonging, there on Pieter's blanket by the river, tipsy and tired and wet. This will be the moment I understand that outrunning my attachments is futile because, wherever I go, I'll just make more, though the pictures Hans sends me months later will tell me I lost traction weeks before this. In one, I'm grinning as Tomas sticks his tongue out at me in Fish River Canyon; in another, taken over a dinner of *gemsbock* in Windhoek, I'm howling as Christo holds two gnawed ribs to the corners of his mouth like tusks; in yet another, I'm beside a campfire in Swakopmund, my hair illuminated by the light of the flash, dancing to the music Pieter always plays from the cab.

Ahead of us lies Botswana – elephants playing in the river, hippos that wonk and squawk and wiggle their ears when Pieter calls to them in what can only be their language – and then Zimbabwe – the Zambezi river crashing and roaring, where, when we finally arrive, we won't be able to see the Victoria Falls for the mist. And as each new campsite moves us closer and closer to the end of our time together, we will begin to press our addresses into each other's palms, promising we will keep in touch, promising we will see one another again, promising we'll all be friends for life.

And in the final hours of our trip, where we drag ourselves up the steps of the truck for the last time to make the all-night push back to Cape Town, Pieter will promise us something too. Tonight, he will tell us, he can make time stand still. If he drives west fast enough on the N1, the sun will not set, and so I will lean my head against Hans's shoulder, and he will lean his head on mine, and we will watch the sun as it hovers on the horizon for hours, watch as Pieter edges the speedometer up and up, faster and faster, until the truck shakes, until the wheels waver, until we lose our race with the turning of the globe that even he can't stop.

Moulting

For a month, it had been all the local newscasters could talk about. The cicadas were coming. Every seventeen years the insects hijacked the city, creating chaos everywhere – drains that clogged and flooded, eves that overflowed when it rained, cars that slammed into each other because the cicadas left puddles the size of a tall man's footprints when they splattered on your windshield. They got snarled in your hair, flew into your mouth if you weren't careful, woke you up at the crack of dawn with their singing if you left your windows open in the springtime heat.

Miranda had lived through the cicadas once before, and was not exactly happy about their return. In fact, nobody seemed happy about it except Mortimer Finch, a biologist who had an office across the hall from Miranda at the small college where she'd taught English for nine years, and who, since March, had spoken of nothing else. Morty was a small, wiry man who kept a pet iguana in his office which he called Bernice, and when he spoke of the creature – "Bernice has a short temper" or "You should have seen the mess Bernice got into today" – people who didn't know Morty sometimes thought it was an unruly wife he was referring to instead of the three-foot reptile plastered to the wall of his office.

Morty often mismatched his clothing, and today's outfit was no exception: green corduroys with a maroon cardigan paired with a yellow-and-white striped shirt. And while Miranda waited for him to get off the phone so they could head over to the weekly meeting of the Curriculum Committee, she began the little game she sometimes played with Morty's clothes, pairing the tan slacks he'd had on yesterday with his blue shirt from last week's meeting and the red tie he'd worn to an admissions event last fall to create an ensemble that didn't swear at itself. It didn't make Morty any better-dressed, but it was a nice distraction from Miranda's last class, which had gone badly again. And now, standing in the doorway of Morty's office, she considered what to do about this as Bernice eyed her from behind the drapes. Iguanas, Morty had explained once, did not wag their tails like dogs when they were happy to see you, but Bernice had stopped puffing her throat at Miranda's presence years ago, which Morty assured her meant the same thing.

"People think," Morty told Miranda now as he locked his office and fell into step beside her, "that cicadas only live for a month or two, but they spend seventeen years underground in the juvenile stage."

"Really," Miranda said.

"Really," Morty said, pushing his glasses up his nose. "We only see them *after* they've tunneled up from underground and climbed the trees to moult. They stay up there until they're ready to shed their skins and mate."

"That's fascinating," Miranda said, who, after nine years, was used to Morty's ramblings, and encouraged, Morty began to explain that the cicadas had already begun the tunneling process when Louellen from Psychology caught up to them and interrupted the dissertation Morty had been about to give on how cicadas lay their eggs.

"You know he's in love with you," Louellen said afterward, as they walked back to the building together.

"Morty?" Miranda asked.

"Yes, *Morty*," Louellen said. "He has been for years. Why don't you give him a chance?"

Miranda thought for a second. "He tells me weird stories."

"About what?"

"Black Widows eating their mates. The ritual courtship of bees." She paused. "There was one about fruit flies I won't even go into."

"Maybe he's flirting with you," Louellen said. "Has it been so long that you don't even know when someone is flirting with you?"

"You're one to talk," Miranda said.

"Yeah, well," Louellen said. "At least I had that thing with Bob in the mailroom last year."

"You mean Bill," Miranda said.

"Right," Louellen said.

But Louellen hadn't been wrong about Miranda. It *had* been that long. And as Miranda drove home from work, she thought about Morty. The truth was that it was not really Morty, or even his stories, she objected to – in fact, she had always liked Morty, his earnestness, his zeal for the daily habits of all ilk of flora and fauna. It was more that Miranda had always been practical about matters of the heart. Men, she'd realized early on, gave you nothing but a mild sort of depression after the dates and phone calls petered out and you were left with a vague memory of having once been giddy about someone you now disliked. And who needed it? So for years she had managed to avoid the whole mess by developing a shield of cultivated ignorance, as if she didn't know what was happening when a barista stopped mid-order during rush hour to deliver her standard cappuccino, or a handyman showed up at her apartment to fix the broken shower curtain but hung around to fix those sagging cupboard doors for free, or a delivery man stood on her doorstep after she'd signed for her parcel, talking about the unseasonably cold weather and grinning like an idiot.

Mostly, Miranda did not think about what she might be missing except on Valentine's Day or Christmas or New Year's Eve, though once, last year, she had been stopped at a street light when a young woman got out of the passenger's side of the car in front of her and walked around to the the driver's side where the young man driving got out, and just before he turned over the keys to her and darted across the street, he had kissed her full on the mouth. Miranda had felt that kiss down to her bones, and sat behind the wheel with her heart fluttering until a car behind her beeped when the light turned green.

But no. Miranda realized early on that sinking energy into men almost never paid off, while sinking energy into studying – and later, teaching – usually did. And now the wall of her office at the college was covered in degrees, and she taught eight classes a year, classes that were dependable in a way that men generally weren't, in that what you put into them, you usually got out of them. Odds were that a solid lesson plan resulted in a lively class discussion, a good one-on-one meeting with a student produced a polished term paper, and a successful semester culminated in a pile of impressive exam results, sometimes even little thank-you cards, Christmas ornaments, and once, a fountain pen engraved with her name. Plus, with teaching, you always got to be in charge. When you told students to do something – take out paper or a pencil or their textbooks – they actually *did it*, unlike men, who looked at you like they'd think about it, maybe, if you asked them to turn down the music or pick you up at 6:00 or come with you to the hospital when you got really sick.

It was only recently that teaching had started to feel different to her. The semester had started off well enough, but now, as it drew to a close, it was her star pupil, Shane McDonnell, who had changed things for Miranda. At first, he'd shown up every day, having done the day's reading not once, but often twice or three times, who spoke brilliantly about Henry James and Edith Wharton, who stopped by her office after class to continue their conversations on Bret Hart, who had written a paper on Jack London that was so brilliant that Miranda had been certain he was destined for graduate school. But one day he hadn't shown up for class, and one day had turned into two, then three, and when he finally returned, unshaven and distracted, he didn't bother bringing his textbook with him, didn't answer questions in class, didn't stop by her office. And then today, he hadn't turned in his assignment on William Dean Howells.

And now Miranda did not know what to do. Usually it was the students you'd identified early as a lost cause who did things like this, but she had not expected it from Shane. He was so talented, so full of promise, so unlike the students to whom she normally had to give her *you-need-to-withdraw-from-this-class* talk, and she hoped, with some encouragement, that he might still live up to the potential he'd shown early on. Miranda resolved to confront him about this gently the next time the opportunity presented itself.

Which it did that very Friday, when, in the midst of a lecture on Stephen Crane, she noticed, beneath the scruffy hair that covered his ears, a set of earphones. He was listening to *music,* Miranda realized, instead of the lecture, and she wondered how long this had been going on. She was so shocked by this discovery that instead of confronting him privately, as she'd planned, she waved to get his attention.

"Shane," she said. "What's with the earphones?"

"WHAT?" he asked, in the too-loud voice people wearing them often used.

"THE EARPHONES?" she asked again.

But Shane only shrugged.

"You can't use them during class," she said. "Please take them off."

He pulled them from his ears then, slipped them in his pocket, and Miranda turned back to *The Red Badge of Courage*. But she could see Shane glowering in the back row, and when it was time to dismiss the class, Miranda stopped him on his way out.

"Is everything all right?" she asked.

"Yup," he said.

"Are you sure?" she asked. "You didn't hand in your assignment."

"I'm fine," he said, but his eyes were fixed on the hallway beyond her, and even before he donned his earphones and walked out, she could see he had already left her behind.

⁊

That evening, sitting in traffic, Miranda could not wait to get home. Her apartment was the place where she withdrew to think when things were bothering her, and she always looked forward to the moment on Fridays when she closed the door behind her and could spend her weekend grading and prepping for classes uninterrupted, everything in a neat pile on her desk by Sunday evening, ready to go for Monday morning.

But when she finally arrived, dropped her bag in the entryway and hung up her coat, she could not stop thinking about the incident with Shane, which ran through her head on a loop, and for the first time her apartment did not offer the sanctuary she'd expected. It seemed too quiet somehow, so she'd poured herself a glass of wine and switched on the television for background noise, but ended up watching *Access Hollywood*, *Law and Order*, *CSI: Miami*, *Saturday Night Live*. By Sunday afternoon, when an old movie she owned came on, she watched it with all the commercials for four-blade razors and luxury cars she'd never own instead of switching to her own copy, just because it made her feel better to think other people were enjoying it with her somewhere in the blue distance, laughing at the same jokes at the same time, though once when the couple across the hall had actually cracked up at the exact moment that Leslie Neilson said *Of course I'm serious and don't call me Shirley* it made her feel worse instead of better, and on Monday morning she was surprised by how happy she was to see Morty Finch standing in the door of her office.

He'd stopped by to inform her of an unscheduled meeting of the Curriculum Committee that had been called over lunchtime, but added that the cicadas were roosting in the trees, and now he launched into a lecture on male cicada songs. "One is an alarm to ward off predators," he said. "Another is used to discourage competition with other males. And that high-pitched buzzing?" he asked. "A mating song. The females are so programmed to respond to it that they're attracted to almost any buzzing sound you could imagine."

"Like what?" she asked.

"Lawn mowers. Leaf blowers. Blenders, even," he added, and when Miranda felt the band of tightness that had been around her chest all weekend rattle loose with laughter, Morty seemed encouraged, and leaned forward.

"Say," he said, "The cicadas start moulting Friday night, and I'm setting up camp on the quad to watch. You're welcome to join me."

Say. Morty was trying to sound casual. Maybe Louellen was right.

"Let me check my schedule," she said, and Morty, who was already late for his nine o'clock class, ducked out just as Louellen stopped by to see if she'd heard about the meeting.

"I think Morty Finch just asked me out," Miranda told her.

"To do what?" Louellen asked.

"Watch cicadas moult."

"That sentimental fool. What did you say?"

"I said I'd check my schedule."

"In case you have a date with Ben and Jerry?"

"Don't worry," Miranda said. "I'll save you a scoop."

But as it turned out, it was Morty who had the date instead. At the emergency meeting of the Curriculum Committee that afternoon, the chairman announced that he'd need Morty to fly to Minnesota on Friday to attend a meeting on accreditation in the sciences that he'd only just learned about.

"Of course," Morty replied, but something about the way his chin began to wobble, and the way he kept touching it to try and correct this, sliced through Miranda. Morty had waited seventeen years for the cicadas to emerge, and now he was going to be stuck in Minnesota.

When the meeting ended, Miranda put her hand on his arm on their way out the door.

"I'm so sorry, Morty," she told him. "Is there anything I can do?"

"No," he began to say, but his voice cracked, and for the first time in the nine years she had known him, Morty Finch was speechless.

But it was Miranda who was speechless when, later that day, Shane McDonnell showed up to class yet again with his earphones on. Miranda had been in the middle of dissecting the last chapter of *The Red Badge of Courage* when she heard the faint sound of music coming from his direction, and she had the urge to walk over and snatch them from his head, which she willed herself not to do, though she could feel her cheeks flushing when she asked him, once more, to remove them. But he had done something then that Miranda had never experienced before in nine years of teaching.

He said, "No."

Miranda was aghast. *No.* Just like that. She did not know how long she stood before the class, her mouth hanging open, only that she had the sudden sense that the other students knew it was too long before she finally found her voice.

"Well, then," she told him, "You can leave."

But he leaned back and said, "I'm not leaving."

"Yes," Miranda said, "you *are.*"

"I'm *not* leaving," he told her. "I pay to be here. You can't make me leave."

And Miranda, who did not know what to do next, who had never before faced such a shocking turn of events, and who – Shane was right about this – could not actually *make* him leave – turned back to the students and Stephen Crane, though she was so flooded with anger that when she returned to the lecture she had trouble remembering where she had been when Shane's earphones had distracted her, and the discussion dragged until class was over.

When she reached her car that evening, Miranda tried to reassure herself that it was not that she was unprepared for Shane's behavior. That she had done the best she could under the circumstances. That there was nothing else she could have done. But by the time she reached the Market Basket, where she shopped every Monday to avoid the crowds, her hands were shaking, and she kept forgetting where things were, and by the time she'd made her way down the frozen foods aisle to the fish counter, where she ordered her salmon steak from the butcher, she was on the verge of tears.

"Just the one?" he asked.

It was then that Miranda truly began to cry.

On her way into the city to give her final exams, the newscasters announced that the cicadas would finally appear the next morning, and Miranda thought of Morty, stuck in Duluth for the very evening he'd been anticipating for years. And she felt so sorry for him as she drove, and for everybody. It really took so little, she thought, to make people happy.

Miranda herself had had a terrible week. Shane's outburst on Monday had been bad enough, but when she arrived in class on Wednesday, it wasn't so much Shane that was the problem. It was more that she detected a kind of vague disrespect from the other students. They stared out the window instead of participating, kept their books closed on their desks, packed up their backpacks long before the class was over, and Miranda tried to remember if this was normal, if it was merely the usual spring fever that overtook them all in early May. But she could not help but suspect that her confrontation with Shane the week before had revealed to her students that at the end of the day, Miranda, for all the energy she poured into teaching, for all her years of experience, for all the letters after her name, had no real authority whatsoever. And for the first time in her career, when they approached her desk to turn in their final exams that afternoon, Miranda felt nothing but relief as she watched them walk out the door for the last time.

She was so glad to see them go, in fact, that she decided to hunker down in her office to read their exams and hand in their final grades that very afternoon so she could put the semester behind her. And she did, just minutes before the registrar's office closed, in return for which she had been handed the anonymous evaluations the students filled out earlier that week, evaluations that, in the past, she had always enjoyed reading. Which is why, in spite of the fact that it was getting late, she brewed herself a cup of tea and began to read through them.

There were the bevy of suggestions about textbook selection, some ideas for improving assignments, and even some nice comments about Miranda herself, though these did not comfort her this time the way they normally did. And now she held in her hands the one she was certain had been written by Shane. She had expected a tirade from him, something easily identifiable. And this was identifiable, except that all he'd written was one short sentence all in caps, traced and retraced in pencil so it stood out gray and shiny on the paper.

It read, *GET A LIFE.*

Miranda held the paper for a long time. She looked at his words, thought about the semester and what had gone wrong, and what she was going to do with the months ahead. In years past she'd always spent her summers organizing her notes, touching up her lesson plans and tweaking her assignments in response to her evaluations in preparation for the fall semester. But now, those hot months seemed to yawn before her like a void, and as she took off her reading glasses and looked out her window at the grassy quad, which was nearly empty in the twilight, she didn't have the faintest idea what she was going do with them.

It was dark outside when Miranda heard a knock on her office door. When she looked up, she was surprised to find Morty standing there, a blanket in one hand and a camera in the other.

"I thought you were in Duluth," she said.

"I paid two thousand bucks for the earliest flight back," he told her. "I'm not going to miss tonight for anything."

And the next morning, when Miranda woke up beside him on the blanket he'd spread beneath the giant old maple tree on the quad the night before, she could see the little bugs everywhere, their tender green bodies now freed of their hulls, right on the cusp of bursting into their calamitous summer song.

A Note about the Author

Photo courtesy of Joshi Radin, © 2013

Mary Elizabeth Pope was raised in Mt. Pleasant, Michigan. She holds a B.S. and M.A. in English from Central Michigan University, and a Ph.D. in English and Creative Writing from the University of Iowa, and currently lives in Boston, Massachusetts, where she is Associate Professor of English at Emmanuel College. Her short stories and essays have been featured in literary magazines such as *Florida Review*, *Bellingham Review*, *PoemMemoirStory*, *Passages North*, and many others. A Michigan native, she spends her summers writing on the Leelanau Peninsula.

OTHER BOOKS FROM WAYWISER

FICTION
Gregory Heath, *The Entire Animal*
Gabriel Roth, *The Unknowns**
Matthew Yorke, *Chancing It*

ILLUSTRATED
Nicholas Garland, *I wish ...*
Eric McHenry and Nicholas Garland, *Mommy Daddy Evan Sage*

NON-FICTION
Neil Berry, *Articles of Faith: The Story of British Intellectual Journalism*
Mark Ford, *A Driftwood Altar: Essays and Reviews*
Richard Wollheim, *Germs: A Memoir of Childhood*

POETRY
Al Alvarez, *New & Selected Poems*
Chris Andrews, *Lime Green Chair*
George Bradley, *A Few of Her Secrets*
Robert Conquest, *Blokelore & Blokesongs*
Robert Conquest, *Penultimata*
Morri Creech, *Field Knowledge*
Morri Creech, *The Sleep of Reason*
Peter Dale, *One Another*
Erica Dawson, *Big-Eyed Afraid*
B. H. Fairchild, *The Art of the Lathe*
David Ferry, *On This Side of the River: Selected Poems*
Jeffrey Harrison, *The Names of Things: New & Selected Poems*
Joseph Harrison, *Identity Theft*
Joseph Harrison, *Someone Else's Name*
Joseph Harrison, ed., *The Hecht Prize Anthology, 2005-2009*
Anthony Hecht, *Collected Later Poems*
Anthony Hecht, *The Darkness and the Light*
Carrie Jerrell, *After the Revival*
Rose Kelleher, *Bundle o' Tinder*
Mark Kraushaar, *The Uncertainty Principle*
Matthew Ladd, *The Book of Emblems*
Dora Malech, *Shore Ordered Ocean*
Eric McHenry, *Potscrubber Lullabies*
Eric McHenry and Nicholas Garland, *Mommy Daddy Evan Sage*

*Co-published with Picador